# LONDON EYE

TIM LEBBON

# LONDON EYE

BOOK ONE

an imprint of Prometheus Books
Amherst, NY

Published 2012 by Pyr®, an imprint of Prometheus Books



Cover illustration © Steve Stone
Jacket design by Nicole Sommer-Lecht

Inquiries should be addressed to
Pyr
59 John Glenn Drive
Amherst, New York 14228–2119
VOICE: 716–691–0133
FAX: 716–691–0137
WWW.PYRSF.COM

16 15 14 13 12 5 4 3 2 1

Library of Congress Cataloging-in-Publication Data

Lebbon, Tim, 1969–
London eye / by Tim Lebbon.
p. cm. — (Toxic city : bk. 1)
ISBN 978–1–61614–680–1 (hardcover)
ISBN 978–1–61614–681–8 (ebook)
1. London (Eng.)—Fiction. 2. Terrorism—Fiction. I. Title.

PS3612.E245L66 2012
813'.6—dc23

2012018464

Printed in the United States of America

*For my beautiful daughter, Ellie*

Huge thanks to my wonderful agent Howard Morhaim,
and my splendid editor Lou Anders.

"The tide of evolution carries everything before it, thoughts no less than bodies, and persons no less than nations."

—*George Santayana, 1863–1952*

# CHAPTER ONE
# CAMP TRUTH

There has been an explosion at the London Eye. Two fatalities are reported, though details are still sketchy. Scotland Yard has issued a brief statement: "There is no indication that this was a terrorist attack." More soon.

*—BBC News Website, 4:34 p.m. GMT, July 28, 2019*

Even though their movements describe a strange, hypnotic beauty, she is certain that the rooks are going to kill her.

She is in the middle of a deserted street. It was silent before, empty, a place she had to herself, though she had been terrified of the silence. Then the peace was broken by the descent of the rooks, and now she is terrified still. She runs for the houses to her right, but though their gates stand open and the front gardens are overgrown and untended, the front doors are all locked tight.

She looks back and up, and the rooks are falling closer. Are they toying with her? Teasing? She cannot say. They circle her in a fast, tight spiral, and she feels as though she is looking into the heart of a black tornado.

Screaming, her voice is lost to the birds, so she decides to run again. Across the street, hands over her ears to block out the rookish cacophony, she stumbles into a burnt-out car, scratching her leg through her jeans. She staggers and falls, feeling tears run from her eyes . . . but she will not show her weakness.

The first of the birds touches her, a gentle stroke of soft feathers across her cheek. She waves her arms but feels nothing. More come down, crowding around her now, claws snagging in her hair, wings beating against her face.

She stands, and this time her scream of rage is heard. *This is not the way for me to go!* She snatches a bird from the air and throws, causing a ripple in the wall of black around her.

Through that ripple, a shadow appears. Its movement is nothing like that of a bird. And then she sees it smile.

Lucy-Anne started awake, scanning her surroundings for birds that were not there, and realised she was in Camp Truth. That afternoon when everything was about to change, Jack was there with her.

She sighed and leaned against Jack. He was seventeen but looked three years older. The loss of his parents in London two years before had aged him, and though he wasn't the sort she usually fell for, their grief had brought them close. He had his eyes closed now, but she could see that he was not asleep. When he slept, his worry lines almost vanished.

Camp Truth always comforted her. It was home to photographs, reports, press clippings, testimonies, and artefacts that revealed a thousand lies about the dreadful fate that had befallen London and which could, if successfully exposed, make so many things right. That was why this was the most important place in Lucy-Anne's world. And she never failed to see the painful irony in Camp Truth existing underground.

When they'd been setting it up, the four of them—her, Jack, Sparky and Jenna—had debated whether to try and keep things hidden away, even down here. The decision had been unanimous: if Camp Truth were found, they were all finished, so why not revel in what they were doing? And so there hung a huge mosaic map of London as it once was across one wall, and stuck all over it were dozens of small clear envelopes. Sparky had made a pinboard for the second wall, and here they had pinned random photographs, cuttings and other ephemera they had gathered over the past couple of years, but which they could not place accurately. Most images were blurred, some damaged by the fires intended to destroy them. A few had been hacked from weapon-cameras just before the people in them were blasted to smithereens.

Lucy-Anne yawned, scratching at her scalp. "Sparky and Jenna coming later?" she asked.

"Don't think so," Jack replied, opening his eyes. "Jenna's out with her parents, and Sparky's still working on the car."

Lucy-Anne laughed without humour. "It's almost forty years old, rusting and dead. Why bother?"

"You know why," Jack said softly.

Lucy-Anne laughed again but said no more, and that was her way of admitting that, yes, she did know why. Sparky liked working with the impossible in the hope that it could change things. If that old Ford Capri ever started again and took to the road, perhaps it would mean that, against all odds, his brother was still alive somewhere in London's sad ruin.

Jack sighed.

"What is it?" Lucy-Anne asked.

"Mum and Dad's wedding anniversary tomorrow."

"Oh, hell, I should have remembered." She sat up straight, flushing with dismay at her bad memory, and Jack smiled and shook his head. But his smile turned sad.

"They'd always wanted a weekend in London on their own," he said, and even though Lucy-Anne had heard this a dozen times, she would always listen again. "They were just . . ." He trailed off, and she pulled him into her embrace and hugged him tight.

They'd been together for almost two years. She would always remember the first time they met; she'd been a fifteen-year-old standing on a chair and offering the world out for a fight. They'd gone to the same counselling sessions for orphans of Doomsday—as the destruction of London had become known—and Lucy-Anne had taken it as a chance to rage against the authorities that put them there. *Bloody lying bastards!* were the first words Jack had heard from her mouth. Her hair had been green then, shaved to a half-inch buzz, and the leathers she wore that day were new, creaking, and obviously stolen.

The others in the group had retreated in fear, cried, or simply turned away, and it had taken the three counsellors half an hour to talk her down. She had sat there for the rest of that session, simmering, and swapping cautious glances with this new orphan.

"We should go," Jack said. "Be dark soon."

"It's always dark," Lucy-Anne said, shivering. And in Camp Truth that was true.

Jack led the way up out of the basement. Lucy-Anne followed, and he wondered once again what had become of them. They'd been down in the basement for almost three hours, and there'd been little more than a quick kiss, and then her haunted sleep. A year ago they'd have spent their time doing a lot more. But things had changed between them, and he still tried to persuade himself that it was because they'd moved on from being teenaged lovers to the best of friends.

She was almost seventeen, but sometimes her grief made her look ageless: she'd lost her parents and brother in London. Her current hairstyle was purple spiked, formed into a carefully sculptured I-don't-give-a-damn mess, and her dark jeans and white tee shirt were tattered and ripped. Those rips *weren't* designer, Jack knew. Lucy-Anne had been left with her family's house, but very little else.

"Sun's going down," he said. He stepped through the curtain of clematis they'd trained across the staircase entrance, and the red splash of dusk exploded across his skin.

Lucy-Anne looked cautiously up into the trees, as if expecting to see a cloud of birds descending towards them from any direction. But the trees were silent, and they were alone. "Red sky at night . . ." she began, and Jack went to her side and put his arm around her waist.

"Shall we check the drops on the way back?"

"Yeah!" She perked up, hugging him with both arms and giving him a kiss. He pinched her bum, she gave him a playful slap, and he welcomed the familiar relief at leaving their secret place.

They walked back through the forest towards their village of Tall Stennington, and on the way they checked the places where truth came to find them.

There were thirteen drops—a number not chosen intentionally, but which the four gang members were pleased with—where unknown people would leave them information about London. They checked them all: a hollow fence post, the space between two half-moon shaped stones, another hole in a fallen tree trunk. And it was only at the thirteenth that they found something.

Lucy-Anne dug the tin from beneath a crab apple tree's roots, lifted the small lid, and squealed in delight when she pulled something out. "It's from Jenna!" she said. She fumbled with the white, flower-painted envelope.

"What does it say?" Jack glanced around to make sure they were alone, always fearful that one day this would be a trap, and there would be soldiers waiting for them. He and his friends would fight to the last, but they could not win, and they'd find themselves taken where all the disappeared went. Into the Toxic City itself, some said. Into the heart of dead London.

"Lucy-Anne?"

"Okay, okay." She unfolded the paper and read the note. "It says, 'My house. I have a nice surprise.'"

Jack's eyes grew so wide that Lucy-Anne uttered a short, quiet giggle.

"We should go," he said. 'A nice surprise' was the code the four of them had agreed upon for something earth-shattering.

And as they ran across the open field separating Tall Stennington from the forest, the moon began to emerge from the darkening sky.

# CHAPTER TWO
# A NICE SURPRISE

*Breaking News:* A suspected gas attack in Central London has left hundreds dead or injured. Hospitals have been put on Major Incident alert. UK Threat Level raised to Critical. Homeland Security Threat Level raised to Severe/Red. More soon.

—*CNN, 11:58 a.m. EST, July 28, 2019*

Jenna answered the front door, looking excited and scared.

"Come on!" she said. "Sparky's already here."

"How did he get here so quickly?" Lucy-Anne asked.

"I went to his place on my bike. Don't worry, I didn't use the phone." Jenna turned and disappeared back into her house.

"I bet she bloody did," Lucy-Anne said as she stepped over the threshold. "Bet she called him."

Jack shook his head and followed his girlfriend inside. They were all careful, but sometimes she was ready to take caution too far. They always went under the assumption that the authorities listened to all telephone communication, but if any eavesdropper heard a girl calling a boy and saying, *Come over, I have a nice surprise*, it was doubtful they'd press the panic buttons.

He immediately noticed the strange atmosphere inside the house. There was nothing definable, nothing he could put his finger on, but the place had an air of . . . change.

A shadow filled the doorway to the kitchen, and the thunderous voice that followed was familiar to them both. "Hey, you bastards, finished playing with each other long enough to join us?"

"Hey, Sparky," Jack said, smiling. They'd become friends through circumstance, brought together because of their beliefs and suspicions, but Sparky was a boy Jack would have got on with anyway, even if Doomsday hasn't happened and London was still there. Sure, he had a wildness about him. Sometimes he acted as if he had a fault-line running along his spine. One day he'd blow. Sparky's brother had blown long before Doomsday, taking to drugs, stealing cars, and running with a gang in the suburbs of London. But Jack was confident that Sparky would keep it together. If he ever did quake, it would be on the shoulders of someone that deserved it.

"Sparky," Lucy-Anne said, "I *never* play." Her false-seriousness made them all laugh, but something about Sparky's mirth sounded different.

"What is it?" Jack asked.

His friend stepped into the hallway. He was sweating, short blond hair pasted to his forehead. His eyes were wide and wild, and Jack thought he'd never seen the boy this worked up. "Something you've got to see for yourselves."

Jenna appeared behind him in the kitchen doorway, short and slight, and wearing her beautiful long dark hair in its usual twisted mess on the back of her head. "You guys coming, or what?"

"Where are your parents?" Lucy-Anne asked.

"They went out. Come on!" Jenna turned and went back into the big kitchen-diner at the rear of the house. Sparky pressed himself against the wall and gestured for them to follow, bowing slightly.

As Jack walked past his big friend they swapped glances, and Sparky's eyes were alight.

There was an old woman sitting in a chair at Jenna's kitchen table. A pot of tea, several used cups, and crumbed plates cluttered the table's surface. The woman looked up and smiled. There was nothing particularly outlandish about the way she was dressed. She had grey, unkempt hair, heavy boots which looked as though they'd suit Lucy-Anne better, old clothes that had seen better days. But a vivid red scar above one eye gave her a wild look. And her smile hid a deep sadness.

"Hello," the woman said. "My name's Rosemary, and I'm from London."

Jack shook his head and backed against the wall. *No one comes out of London*, he thought. *They shoot the things that try. They* burn *them!*

Rosemary's smile grew. "Don't believe everything you see in the media. But then, you're the last people I need to say that to."

"Did you . . . read my mind?" Jack asked.

"No, not me," Rosemary said, "although I know a young woman back in the city who can do just that."

"Isn't it wonderful?" Jenna asked. She stared at Jack and Lucy-Anne, as if expecting her enthusiasm to wash over them as well.

"Bloody miracle, is what it is," Sparky said.

"How did you get out?" Jack asked.

Rosemary took a glass from the kitchen table and sipped at the water it contained. She closed her eyes and sighed; the sweetest thing ever. "Tunnels. There's a whole network under London, and not all of them are guarded."

Jack shook his head. It didn't make sense. "So why haven't more people come out before now?"

"The route's only just been found. There's a man called Philippe who can see the lie of the land. A three-dimensional map in his mind, that's how he explains it to me, and he discovered this way to escape the city. We're afraid that a larger escape would be spotted, so I came alone to meet Jenna's father."

"Why?" Jack was still pressed against the wall, and he felt his friends' eyes on him; Jenna angry, Sparky challenging, Lucy-Anne . . . he could not read her. She was a blank. He hoped it was caution.

"So many questions," Rosemary said.

"What the bloody hell do you expect?"

"Jack," Jenna said, stepping forward. She touched his shoulders and looked up at him. She was sweet, her caramel skin impossibly smooth, and in other circumstances he could have seen them being together. But she was usually so filled with sadness that she rarely let anyone close.

"It's just something I never expected."

"It's something we've always *hoped* for!" Jenna whispered.

"So what can you do?" he asked over his friend's shoulder.

"I'm a healer," Rosemary said.

"Huh!"

Jenna squeezed his arms, but he would not catch her eye. *She could have been sent here by the Capital Keepers*, he wanted to say. And the more he thought about that, the more likely it seemed. If that were the truth they were already doomed, and they'd be whisked away, and even if they *were* allowed back home they'd be changed like Jenna's father. Ghosts of their former selves.

"Need an open mind, mate," Sparky said.

Jack shook his head. "It just can't be."

Jenna sighed, and rested her head on his shoulder to whisper into his ear. The closeness surprised him. "Always the doubter," she said.

And then she stabbed him.

Lucy-Anne went for Jenna. The girl turned with the knife held out. Lucy-Anne feinted right, then moved left, swinging her forearm before her to divert Jenna's arm. But the knife fell and struck the tiled floor with a splash of blood, and Jenna retreated against the closed back door.

Lucy-Anne snatched up the blade and was on the other girl in a second. She pressed her against the door with an arm across her throat, and then they locked stares; two friends who had been through so much, and Lucy-Anne remembered a dozen times when they had eased each other's tears.

"What the hell . . . ?" she asked, and Jenna shook her head.

"Lucy-Anne, trust me."

Lucy-Anne looked down at where Jack had slumped to the floor. He was pale, but for the startlingly bright blood pulsing between his fingers from his leg. *Artery*, she thought, *oh shit, she got his artery*. She glanced across at where a phone was fixed to the wall.

Rosemary rose from the table, sighing as her joints clicked with audible pops. "Don't worry," she said, her voice endlessly calm.

"Don't worry?" Lucy-Anne shouted. She pulled Jenna from the door and pushed her across the kitchen towards the old woman, facing them all with the bloodied knife held before her. "Don't *worry*?" She looked at Sparky, expecting support from him but seeing only a strange, subdued excitement in his eyes. He was not looking at her, or the knife she held, or even at their friend bleeding to death on the floor. He was looking at Rosemary.

Jack groaned. He was staring down at his leg, watching as pressure pumped the blood past his pressing hands.

Rosemary stood by Jack's feet and looked at Lucy-Anne. "Girl, I'll give you a reason to believe," she said, and then she knelt beside the wounded boy. Jack tried to wave her away, but his coordination was failing.

"Let her," Jenna said.

Lucy-Anne watched. Her own heart was beating in time with Jack's pulsing blood, and she held the knife so tight that her fingers hurt. *I won't let go*, she thought. *Not until I'm sure*. But she was holding the knife on her best friends in the world, and something about that made her feel sick.

Rosemary lifted Jack's hands away from his wound, and used a small pair of scissors to cut open his sodden jeans. Then she replaced his hands with her own. She gave him a quick, sad smile, and then her eyes closed. Her face went blank—*empty*—as though she had gone elsewhere.

And then her hands slipped inside Jack's leg.

When Jack came to, Jenna was on her hands and knees mopping up the blood, but she could not take her eyes off the old woman. Rosemary sat at the kitchen table again, drinking water and sighing as though it were nectar.

"Do you actually fix it, or is it, like . . . ?" Lucy-Anne trailed off. She was sitting opposite the old woman. She had a knife in her left hand, resting on her leg, and as she shifted it fell to the floor. She did not seem to notice.

"Hey . . ." Sparky lifted the short sleeve of his tee shirt exposing the tattoo of his brother's name that he'd done himself. He'd been drunk at the time, and the 'S' of Stephen looked more like an 'F.' "Can you fix this?"

Rosemary smiled and shook her head.

"How about this?" Sparky pointed at his face.

Rosemary frowned. "What's wrong with it?"

"Ugly," Jack said, and it seemed to take all his energy. Here he was, subject of a miracle, and everyone's attention was elsewhere. But when he looked at his leg at last—and saw the smooth spread of skin that minutes earlier had been pouting open—he realised that he was wrong. He was not the miracle at all.

"So do you now believe, non-believer?" Jenna roared, her voice mock-deep. Jack stood cautiously, leaning against the wall. He put weight on his leg. It felt as though the wound had never been there at all.

"You stabbed me."

"Well . . ." She shrugged, raising her eyebrows.

"Yeah," Jack said. "I believe."

"So can we all talk now?" Jenna asked. She sat at the table and motioned the others to join her.

*This is it*, Jack thought. *This is when it all changes. I've been touched already, but if we sit and listen to this woman, we'll get drawn in*. Rosemary smiled at him, inviting him to join them at the table, and in that moment he saw something of his mother in her. She was much older than his mum—maybe seventy-five—and weary, worn by time and circumstance. But she exuded a deep-set goodness from every pore.

"Does it hurt to heal?" Jack asked. That question suddenly seemed very important.

"No," she said. "It feels as natural as breathing."

Jack nodded, went to the table and sat down next to Lucy-Anne. She grabbed his hand and squeezed too hard, her nervousness and excitement obvious. Sometimes he sensed such violence in her that it scared him.

"So why have you come for my father?" Jenna asked.

"Things are falling apart," Rosemary said. She sighed, and looked around the table. "How much do you all know?"

"We know it wasn't terrorists," Jack said. "An army scientist crashed a helicopter into the London Eye and released a virus they called Evolve."

"Angelina Walker," Jenna said. "No one knows why she did it."

Jack nodded. "We know that not everyone in London was infected and killed."

"And that the survivors are hunted," Jenna added.

"And they're special," Lucy-Anne said. "They're called Irregulars, like you."

"Not all like me," Rosemary said. "I can heal. Others can do different things, a whole host of *amazing* things. And we're all sought-after by the Choppers."

"Choppers?"

"That's what *we* call the ones that hunt us. You call them Capital Keepers. But whether they're scientists or military, it doesn't really matter. When they catch an Irregular they do . . . terrible things. So we call them Choppers."

"What terrible things?" Lucy-Anne asked, squeezing Jack's hand even harder.

Rosemary closed her eyes. "We need help. We need to get out of there, and the only way that will happen without slaughter is if the general public—*all* of them—know the truth of what's happening. We need exposure." She looked at Jenna. "That's why I came to find your father. To ask him to come in with me, gather evidence, and then present it to the world. So . . . will he be here soon?"

"It's *us* you're talking to here!" Lucy-Anne said. She stood sharply, sending her chair scraping across the floor. "And don't you bloody *dare* look down on us just because we're just kids. We've all grown up a lot since Doomsday, because we've *had* to." She pointed at Jack. "Mother and father." At Sparky. "Brother." And herself. "Mother, father, brother."

Rosemary's expression did not change at this roll-call of the missing and dead. "The last thing I'd call you is kids," she said.

Lucy-Anne nodded, seemingly satisfied. When she sat down she held Jack's hand again, but this time it was a gentle touch.

"My dad's out with Mum," Jenna said. "They go walking a lot. Sometimes they take me, but usually I just want to stay at home. We didn't lose anyone. But Dad . . ."

"He fought," Rosemary said.

"Yeah." Jenna nodded, staring past them all. "Looked for the truth. First they called him an activist, and threatened him with the law. When he ignored their threats, they took him."

"He was in contact with several people in London," Rosemary said. "People who could enhance their brainwaves to such an extent that they almost acted as radio transmitters and receivers."

"'Could'?" Sparky asked.

"When the Choppers discovered the communication, they took all three. Beheaded two of them in the street, so the word goes, and the other just disappeared. Camp H."

"'H' for what?" Lucy-Anne asked.

"Hope," Rosemary said with a wry smile.

"That was the same time they took Dad?"

"Yes. But we don't think they bring outsiders to Camp H."

"He never told us where he went," Jenna said, "or who took him, or what they did to him. When he left, he was so full of fight and anger. Every time I kissed him goodnight, there was a real power about him. He had purpose. He came back two weeks later and . . ." She opened her hand like a quickly blooming flower. "Pff. Gone. Sometimes I can't believe he's still my dad." The volume of her voice had grown, but the tears came as well, and Jenna shook with anger and grief.

"Then I suppose he can't help me anymore," Rosemary said sadly.

"Is it true they implant something?" Sparky said. "When they take people and send them back. Something to kill them if they start investigating again?"

Rosemary shrugged slowly. "How can I know that? This is your world out here. I live in London, but that's a whole new world now."

"You've heard of it though, right?" Jack asked.

"Rumours."

"And you still came to ask him for help?"

Rosemary stared at him then, and Jack was certain she was trying to convey some message that she did not wish to voice. He stood, let go of Lucy-Anne's hand and walked to the kitchen sink.

Outside, the sunset was burning across the ridges of neighbouring houses. Jenna's parents would be back soon.

"I need to know," Jack said quietly.

"Me too," Sparky said.

Lucy-Anne stood and ran her hands through her purple hair. "Yeah."

Jack turned back and looked at Rosemary; an old woman, worn and tired, scarred and grubby, but filled with an astonishing power that the government had gone to brutal measures to conceal.

"*We'll* come," he said.

Rosemary nodded slowly and smiled. "The second you were all here together, I knew that would happen."

"Another power?" Jenna asked. "You're an empath?"

"No, dear," the old woman laughed. "I'm human."

They split up, agreeing to meet at Camp Truth at dawn the following morning. Jenna and Sparky were taking Rosemary there to sleep. They said it was probably the safest place of all, but the old woman seemed too tired to be afraid.

She scared Lucy-Anne. There was something . . . different about her. There was that incredible thing she had done with Jack's leg, yes, but she seemed so very out of place here in the village. She sat at Jenna's table and drank tea, ate toast, talked to them and fended their questions, but to Lucy-Anne it seemed as if she were from another world.

In a way, she supposed that was true.

Jack had been keen to get home to his sister Emily, so Lucy-Anne had walked home alone. She'd stopped in the corner shop and bought a bottle of cheap red wine, joking with the boy behind the counter who flirted with her every time she went in. He was her age but seemed so much younger, and she thought it was because he'd lost no one to Doomsday. He seemed happy and content, and blissfully unaware of what had gone on in his world because so little of it had touched him. Sometimes she thought of inviting him home to see if some of his carefree attitude would rub off on her. But she knew that she'd end up showing him pictures, and talking about those she had lost, so she'd left him with a smile and a sway of her hips.

Sitting in the living room of the big, empty house left to her when her family had vanished in the Toxic City, Lucy-Anne allowed the tears to come. Usually they were driven by grief and sadness, but today there was something else: the terror that soon, all her fears would be realised.

She had never, ever let herself accept the fact that they were dead.

She swigged from the bottle. It was half gone already, and she knew she should pour the rest down the sink. Last thing she wanted tomorrow was a hangover. But she was enjoying the fuzziness in her head, and it seemed to relax her muscles, enabling her to sink into the sofa and lose herself in the music blasting from her stereo.

"Sorry, Mum and Dad!" she called up to their bedroom. Led Zeppelin was particularly loud this evening, and she knew they didn't like it very much.

She never went into their room, and kept the door locked.

"Andrew, you always did like good music!"

Her brother's bedroom door was locked as well, but she had not felt able to remove his favourite CDs from where he'd left them scattered around the music system in the living room. Now they were her favourites, too.

She drank a little more, and spoke to her family, because this was the only place and time she would ever allow herself to do so: at home, alone, when no one could see her true desperation.

Tomorrow, everything was going to change.

It looks like a huge, open wasteland, but she can see its ghosts.

There used to be buildings here, and parks, and shops and pubs where people had mixed and chatted, laughing and scowling their way through life. It has all gone now, and their absence seems to make the sky far too large.

Instead there is a vast plain of broken rubble, exotic-looking plants and flattened, blurred areas that look so strange. She sees movement far away across the plain, and she squints into the merciless sun, shading her eyes to see whether it's people . . . or something else.

She walks towards the movement because it seems the best place to go. It's hot and harsh here, with a warm breeze blowing from the left and carrying a melange of scents: the dust of ages; dry, old rot; and something spicy and forbidden which she cannot identify.

As she nears the thing she saw moving, she finally makes out what it is. The pack of wolves is rooting at something buried deep in the ground. It's one of those strange blurred areas that she had seen, and she can now identify that effect as well: in this rugged plain of a dead city, this spread of land is as smooth as a bowling green.

The wolves growl, but she walks closer. She thought she had a knife in her pocket, still stained with the blood of a friend, but she frowns when she finds her pocket empty. Maybe she dropped it? She feels like a fool, because there are so many dangers out here.

She should be scared of the wolves, but she is not here for them. So she shouts and they flee, casting incongruous growls back as they disappear among the rubble.

The sky darkens as she walks out onto the flattened area. The breeze dies down, but she can smell rot well enough. And even though the sun has hidden its face behind a cloud, the glare of unearthed bones is obvious.

She kicks through the bones, hauling skeletons aside, rifling through half-rotten clothing, shouting out for her mother, father, and brother. She's desperate not to find them, but she cannot tear herself away.

And then there are her parents, dead but not rotten, buried deep down where the wolves had not reached, and there are worms in their eyes and beetles in their mouths, and even as she looks to the sky and screams she can see them still.

She will know them like this forever.

# CHAPTER THREE
# ANNIVERSARY

It is now believed that the explosion at the London Eye was a terrorist attack. Following the explosion, a toxic agent has been released into the atmosphere. Deaths have been reported in Westminster, Chelsea, Bayswater, Mayfair, and West Kensington. Security Services are closing off large tracts of south and west London, and residents are advised to **remain indoors, close all windows and doors,** and **await further instructions**. Please do not attempt to leave the city. More soon.

—*BBC News Website, 5:15 p.m. GMT, July 28, 2019*

Next morning, Jack and his sister Emily headed for Camp Truth. Rucksacks over their shoulders, they were walking into the sunrise and beginning a journey leading somewhere Jack had dreamed of for two years.

He felt that rush of youthful anticipation—part wonder, part fear—that had been absent for so long. But above that even now hung the crushing weight of his responsibility. He had Emily to look after and look out for, a young girl who sometimes had trouble remembering her parents' faces when she was tired, crying and needing them most. Jack was always there for her, offering a hug and trying to hold back his own tears because he was the grown-up now. He was the one who played with Emily and told her off, washed her clothes and helped with her school work, prepared her meals and looked after the house. He sobbed with her sometimes, but other times he had to scold her if she misbehaved. He'd tried to tell himself that not tidying her room when he asked was too insignificant to worry about, but the gravity of Doomsday sometimes seemed to exaggerate the smallest of things.

Emily skipped on ahead, her rucksack bouncing on her back. She held her digital camera in one hand, fully charged the previous evening, strap wrapped around her wrist three times. Mum had bought it for her, and she'd treasured it ever since. Jack had lost count of the number of DVDs Emily had filled with random still and moving images, all of them seemingly meaningless but meaning the world to her.

They reached the edge of the village, and as they passed by the dilapidated old scout hut Jack felt nothing. He'd grown up in Tall Stennington, had many good times there—making mud pies at the village pond with his cousin when he was six; playing baseball on the green as his parents sat outside the pub; seen his first naked breast at twelve when Billy White smuggled him into his older sister's bedroom closet—but the bad far outweighed the good. Crossing the field towards the woods, he felt as if he was truly leaving his childhood behind.

"Don't run, you'll trip!" he called to Emily, and he laughed at the foolishness of his statement. They were heading for London, the Toxic City, where millions had died and the government claimed that monsters now lived. And he was worried about a grazed knee.

"What's wrong?" Emily called back.

Jack could only laugh and splutter some more.

"You sound like a hyena."

He ran after his sister, yapping and barking. She squealed and hurried on, and they were both sprinting as they entered the shadow of the woods, keen to leave the past in the cleansing sunlight.

They took a circuitous route around the edge of the woods, following a path popular with dog walkers and strolling lovers. Jack sometimes walked this way with Lucy-Anne, and a few times they'd gone deeper into the woods, spread a blanket and messed around. But recently there had always been a reason for their messing to end; wood ants on her naked legs, a noise from the bushes, a feeling that they were being watched. And not all the reasons had come from her. Jack tried to put it down to being scared, but it wasn't that, not really. He felt as if he had turned from Lucy-Anne's lover into her best friend, but he was not certain she thought that way. One day they'd have to talk about things, but she was such a strange girl; sometimes she scared him.

And sometimes, he knew, he just thought about things too damn much.

*Clothes, water, food.* He mentally flipped through the contents of his backpack. *Washing stuff, money, knife.* The beginning of the Exclusion Zone was thirty miles away, but they'd be able to get public transport for more than half that distance. *Medicine, bandages, antibiotics.* Beyond that, they'd walk. Rosemary said she knew where they were going. They'd have to trust her.

When they came close to the burned-down mansion, they paused. Emily had been here a few times, but usually Jack didn't like bringing her to Camp Truth, afraid that the responsibility of keeping the place secret would weigh too heavily on her young shoulders.

Sparky came crashing through the undergrowth. He was red in the face, sweating, and he carried a small rucksack over one shoulder, barely big enough to hold a spare tee shirt and jeans.

"Rosemary's still there," Sparky said.

"Never thought she wouldn't be," Jack replied. "The others here yet?"

"Jenna's just gone down to talk to her. Lucy-Anne's checking the drops on the way in."

Jack watched Emily dash off between the trees towards the ruined house, happy now he knew Jenna was already down in Camp Truth.

"You okay?" he asked his friend.

"'Spose," Sparky said.

"We'll be all right."

"Yeah. Feels like we're doing something at last."

They stood silently for a moment, neither catching the other's eye, each finding something interesting to look at in the woods.

"We could disappear," Jack said quietly. "Have you and your parents . . . ? You know."

"Made peace? Nah. Sod 'em. They never forgave Stephen, even after Doomsday."

"Perhaps they think he doesn't need forgiving if he's dead."

Sparky's face dropped, innocent and honest. "That's just stupid."

Jack nodded. "You'll be fine."

"Thanks, mate. And yeah, I need this. I really do. Otherwise I've got you lot, and the Capri, and . . ."

"It's not inevitable."

"That I'd end up doing what Steve did? Drink, drugs, nicking cars? Nah, not inevitable." But he looked away between the trees, and Jack wondered how close Sparky had already come.

"Has the car started yet?"

"Honestly? I think it's been ready for weeks. I've taken it apart, cleaned it, replaced what I can and put it back together. All the work I'm doing on it now is cosmetic, really. Fixing rust, repainting. But I'm afraid to try. Even yesterday evening, knowing where we're goin'. *Especially* then. I was afraid to try. Last thing I want now is a bad omen."

"Hey, you guys!" Lucy-Anne said. She approached along a narrow path from deeper in the woods, skirting around a pile of rubble from the old house. She seemed excited and breathless. "You'll never guess what I found in one of the drops!"

"A lump of squirrel shit?" Sparky asked.

Lucy-Anne didn't even look at him. Instead she turned and dashed towards the hidden entrance to Camp Truth. "Come on!" she said over her shoulder. Her eyes sparkled, her hair was freshly spiked, and Jack wished that they could have kept things between them stronger.

As Lucy-Anne descended into Camp Truth, she saw Rosemary. *Still real*, she thought, smiling at the idea that she could have ever been a dream.

Rosemary smiled at her, then looked past her shoulder. "Good morning, Jack."

"Sleep okay?" Jack asked.

She nodded, flexing her shoulder slowly. "Old bones, that's all. I've met your little sister. She's wonderful!"

Emily was sitting on one of the tatty chairs they'd brought down here a few months ago, panning slowly around the room with her camera, eyes fixed on the display screen on its back. Lucy-Anne waved and poked her tongue out, and Emily giggled.

"You guys *really* need to see this," Lucy-Anne said. She opened a small white envelope and produced a photograph, and Sparky, Jack, and Jenna gathered behind her. "Picture of someone *in the city*. We've had *nothing* like this before."

"Did you put that there?" Sparky asked the old woman.

Rosemary shook her head.

Lucy-Anne held up the photograph. "Here, you can see a ruined building behind this woman, a burnt out car, and some things . . ." She shivered, a deep, cold feeling, and she knew what her mum would have said: *Someone walking over your grave*. "Dogs," she said. "In a pack." She usually loved dogs, but something about those in the picture haunted her.

The light in Camp Truth was not the best, and the photograph was small. They all leaned in closer, and Lucy-Anne felt the heat and pressure of her friends at her back.

"Got something around her neck . . ." Jenna muttered.

Jack gasped. He tried to speak, but his voice came out as a groan.

Lucy-Anne turned in time to see Sparky throw an arm around their friend, holding Jack up when his legs seemed to fail him.

"What is it, mate?" Sparky asked.

Jack held out his hand, and Lucy-Anne gave him the photograph. He moved carefully away from Sparky, showed Emily, and the little girl burst into tears. Then he held up the photo for them all to see again, and Lucy-Anne scolded herself for not realising before.

"Mum," Jack said. "That's my mum."

# CHAPTER FOUR
# FAMILY OUTING

. . . and the British Government has restricted all movement into and out of London. All airports in the UK have been closed, with over five hundred flights diverted to French, German, and Spanish airports, and more than two hundred turned back to their countries of origin. At this time, the agent used in the attack has not been identified, and it is not known whether it is chemical or biological in origin. Pictures still being transmitted from inside London show soldiers in NBC suits barricading roads, and bodies piled by roadsides. There is no official word on casualties, although an unnamed source inside the Ministry of Defence describes the death toll as "catastrophic." The British prime minister is expected to make a statement shortly.

Homeland Security Threat Level is maintained at Severe/Red, and the American public is asked to be on their guard.

*—CNN, 12:20 p.m. EST, July 28, 2019*

*Mum's still alive.*

The words were fresh in Jack's mind as they left Camp Truth and headed through the woods. Rosemary and Lucy-Anne went as a grandmother and her granddaughter going to visit friends. Sparky and Jenna were pretending to be boyfriend and girlfriend, a prospect which delighted Sparky and seemed to annoy Jenna immensely. And Jack and his sister Emily were on a family outing. If anyone asked where their parents were, Jack would only have to say "dead" for the understanding to hit home, and he hoped someone *did* ask, because *his mother was still alive!*

Emily fluttered around in excitement, filming everything in sight. Jack wanted to tell her to save the batteries, but he knew she had several spares and a solar recharger, and he liked seeing her so absorbed in something. He could always tell the difference between her being simply distracted, or completely involved in something that took her away from their sad reality. Now, she was just a little girl chasing butterflies.

When they emerged from the woods and walked along the main road, traffic was light, and nobody seemed to pay them any attention. A police car zipped by, pale face at the window. Closer to the bus stop, Jack held his breath as a Capital Keeper wagon roared past. It had once been an army truck, but the camouflage paint had gone, replaced by the now-familiar deep Royal Blue.

"I wonder where they've been," Emily said. She was so bright. Most kids her age would have asked where they were going.

Their bus was on time, and they sat halfway along the top deck. The sun beat through the windows and made Jack sweat, but he enjoyed the heat. He looked out and watched the world go by.

He saw a field full of cows, and a car that had been stopped by the police, its occupants made to sit beside the road with their wrists bound while the officers ripped the car apart. He saw a lake where people rode jet skis, and three houses set back from the main road that had been burnt out, their blackened windows looking like sad, cried-out eyes. And amongst the faces staring from cars and lorries passing them by, he saw blank sadness that spoke volumes.

Normality, for these times after Doomsday.

"Mum's still alive," he whispered in Emily's ear, and she grinned.

The journey took a little over an hour, and they were both glad to get off the bus. They weren't used to travelling so far.

They followed the directions Rosemary had given them, watching out for the shop names, and when they passed the Beckham Bistro, they left the pavement and headed down the narrow, rubbish-strewn alley between buildings. At the end of the alley they crossed an area of undeveloped ground. Glass crunched underfoot, and a wild dog barked at them and stalked slowly away. There were lots of wild dogs now—as well as cats, parrots, and snakes—their owners killed in London, and though there were frequent culls, numbers seemed to be increasing. Before Doomsday Jack could remember his father being fascinated with cryptozoology, the study of exotic animals living wild in Britain: wolves, bears, black panthers, cougars, and alligators, all were rumoured to be thriving. He wondered what his dad would make of this.

They crossed the area of rough ground, passed between two blocks of flats that had seen better days, then exited onto the towpath beside a canal.

As they passed beneath a metal road bridge spanning the canal, something changed. It took Jack a moment to spot exactly what it was: everything had grown silent. No more buzzing flies, no rustles in the overgrowth alongside the towpath, no barking from beyond the hedges and walls. It was spooky as hell, and he didn't like it one bit.

"Jack—" Emily began, her voice shadowed with worry.

Someone jumped down from the bridge's underside and pressed something against his back. "Do what I say, or I blow your kidneys all over your shoes."

Jack glanced at Emily, and her face broke into a smile.

"I really wish I'd had my camera ready for that one," she said.

"One of these days, Sparky . . ." Jack said, turning around.

"Yeah?" Sparky was still pointing his finger-and-thumb gun. "You and which army?"

"I thought we were meeting under a viaduct?"

"Just along there," the boy nodded. "Couple hundred yards. I decided to wander back here, make sure we weren't followed, or nothin'."

"Everyone get here okay?"

"Fine." Sparky grinned, rubbing his cheek. "Jenna gave me a right slap on the bus when I tried getting frisky, though."

Jack examined his friend's red, slightly swollen cheek. He nodded. "Good."

"Let's go!" Emily said. She ran along the towpath, scaring several ducks into the water.

"You've got to help me look after her, Sparky," he said quietly.

"You know I will." Sparky slapped the back of Jack's head, hard, and laughed. "But you know something? I think *she'll* be looking after *us*." Behind the laughter he was deadly serious, and Jack reminded himself yet again how blessed he was with friends.

They descended from the towpath down a steep slope, and when they entered the damp shadow of the viaduct Jack felt a chill that had nothing to do with temperature. Rosemary, Jenna, and Lucy-Anne were waiting for them there. Lucy-Anne gave him a nervous smile, but he could see that she was excited, too.

"We're about to leave the world you know," Rosemary said, and Jack's chill seemed to settle into his bones.

The brick arch of the viaduct leaked in several places, raining water down around them and turning the ground into a quagmire. Jack had often wondered what would happen if such a canal bridge were to collapse. Would the whole waterway drain away down here? Would everything in its path be washed away? The red brick was swathed in moss, and from the ruts in the ground it appeared that the leaks had been dripping for a long time.

"It's less than ten miles to the Exclusion Zone from here," Jenna said. "We're walking the rest of the way?"

"Not used to exercise?" Rosemary asked, smiling.

"I *love* walking," Jenna said. "It's just that . . . won't we be seen?"

"Only if people look in all the wrong places. Like I said, we're leaving your world, going somewhere different. Slipping between the lines. It's not a quick journey, but we'll follow paths that will take us all the way into London, undetected and safe."

"And your friend Philippe showed you the way?" Lucy-Anne asked.

"Yes, Philippe. Though he's hardly a friend." Rosemary smiled sadly. "London's not an easy place for friendships right now, I'm sad to say. I do have some, but . . . well, there's so much paranoia."

"So how do you know you can trust him?" Sparky asked.

"I think I'm a good judge of character." Rosemary looked around at the five of them, saving her smile for Emily. Then she pointed away from the viaduct and along an overgrown path that seemed to lead into darkness. "We're going there."

Jack's friends glanced around for a beat, meeting each other's eyes as though waiting for a decision to be made. It was Emily who started after the old woman, glancing back at them all with eyebrow raised.

Sparky started singing. "We're *off* to see the *Wizard*—"

"If you sing any more," Jenna said, "I will kill you in your sleep."

"The *wonderful* Wizard of Oz." Sparky even started skipping.

They followed Rosemary, placing themselves completely in her hands. It was the riskiest thing any of them had done since coming together after Doomsday, but Jack knew it was the *right* thing, as well. They had all been aware that one day, the time for action would arrive.

Very soon, Jack had the real sense that they were travelling just beyond the veil of reality before which most people lived their lives. Rosemary led them through places that seemed forgotten, cast aside or ignored, and sometimes they could hear, and even see the world going on around them. It was like a route leading back from what the world had become towards what it might have been before, though he knew that at the end of this route lay something else entirely: London as it was now; the Toxic City.

The path from the viaduct led between the rear gardens of two rows of abandoned houses. Many of the structures seemed unsafe and close to collapse, and one or two had already taken the first tumble into ruin. One long spread of buildings on their right had been burnt out, roof joists blackened and exposed to the sky. Few windows remained. Gardens were overgrown, and here and there Jack caught sight of children's playthings clogged with bramble and grass, dulled primary colours showing through the green foliage. He wondered why so many houses had been abandoned at once.

The path stopped against a blank brick wall, a tall boundary construction that seemed to close off the garden space between the two terraces. Rosemary waited for them there, then started down a set of steps almost completely overgrown with brambles. She descended silently. At the bottom, surrounded by banks of undergrowth and overshadowed by the high wall, they huddled together before a boarded area at the base of the barrier.

"Old canal route," Rosemary said. "It was drained and decommissioned when they built these houses, over a hundred years ago. It's dark in here. You might want to get your torches out."

"How far does it go?" Jenna asked, amazed.

"This goes out to the edge of town. From there, we go underground almost all the way into the Exclusion Zone."

"Underground how?" Jack asked. While everyone else was taking torches from their rucksacks, he stared at the timber boarding, one rotten corner of it recently detached.

"You'd be surprised," Rosemary said. "There are plenty of places beneath the surface of things." She grabbed the corner of a plywood sheet and tugged, popping it from a couple of loose nails and resting it back against the board beside it. "People have been building in this country for thousands of years. Much of what's underground is unmapped, uncharted, and forgotten. Philippe has the talent to find it, which is something new. I suspect he knows of places that haven't been seen, or trodden by human feet, for many centuries. Canals, underground rivers, storage basements, tunnels, subterranean hiding places, cave networks, roads built over and blocked off."

"Looks spooky," Lucy-Anne said, but Jack could hear the excitement in her voice at the prospect.

"Oh, it's bound to be haunted," Emily said. She had picked the camera from her rucksack, not her torch.

They all stood there for a moment longer, and Jack looked up at the narrow spread of blue sky above them. The sun was behind the brick wall, and he could barely feel the summer heat down here. But he was ready. Darkness, shadows, and secret ways beckoned, but beyond that, the revelations he had been craving for two years.

And his mother. The picture was in his pocket, her stern, beautiful face waiting for him whenever he needed a look. He and Emily had mentioned their father only in whispers, afraid of what their mother's expression might mean.

"I'll go in last," Emily said. "I *really* need to get this." She stood back with her camera, and Rosemary led them away from daylight and into the night.

# CHAPTER FIVE
# OUT OF THIS WORLD . . .

> . . . and the advice is to remain indoors and await further instructions. Government sources state that there is, as yet, no credible claim for responsibility. What is clear is that there has been a massive breakdown of communication into and out of London, with mobile phone networks down, satellite systems malfunctioning, and land lines dead. We understand that the prime minister will be delivering a statement at 6:00 p.m. But as of now, far from becoming clearer, the situation seems to be descending . . . (broadcast ends here)
>
> —*BBC TV Newsflash, 5:35 p.m. GMT, July 28, 2019*

To begin with, Jack was disappointed. They walked along the dried canal bed, their torch lights flashing here and there like reflections from long forgotten water, and on the old towpaths he made out at least a dozen box structures obviously used as temporary shelters by tramps. Smashed booze bottles littered the ground, bags of refuse lay split open by rats or other carrion creatures, and he saw many broken items from the world above. He had believed that they were leaving the world he knew, but it appeared they had merely entered its underside.

But then Jenna called out from where she had stalked ahead with Rosemary, and the excitement kicked back in: "Oh, this is not a nice way to go."

They caught up with her and all trained their torches in the same place. There was a skeleton propped against the side of the dry canal. It still wore the faded remnants of clothing, but the bones had been picked clean, and in places there were what looked like teeth marks. One leg was gone below the knee, and both arms were missing.

"Gross!" Emily said. Jack thought briefly of leading her away, but he would not patronise her like that. They were all seeing this together.

"Some bones over there," Sparky said, pointing with his torch. Jack saw a few loose bones scattered across the ground, splintered and chewed. "Let's just hope he or she was dead before the dogs got to them."

Lucy-Anne walked on quickly, turning her torch from the body and marching ahead into the tunnel. She paused after twenty yards, and Jack could see her shoulders rising and falling as she panted.

"Lucy-Anne?" he asked.

"I'm fine!" But she did not turn around, and when she heard their footsteps she went on alone.

Beyond the skeleton—as though death could be a barrier, or a border—they found very few signs of human interference. Their bobbing torch beams picked out stalactites hanging from the arched ceiling, and in several places water dripped in unavoidable waterfalls. Emily giggled as she ran through and got soaked, but Jack could not help wondering at the water's origin. He hoped for a ruptured water main, not a foul drain.

It was cold, down in this place never touched by sunlight or heat. There was a very slight breeze coming from ahead, and without that Jack guessed the tunnel would have stank. Every few seconds someone's torch beam would illuminate the edge of the dried canal, reminding him of where they were and how strange this was. But though it was dark, and unsettling, and the air went from musty to fresh in a breath, there was a palpable sense of excitement. Jack felt enthused, and he could sense the others experiencing their own versions of the same anticipation. Their fast breathing echoed, torch lights bobbed erratically, and a loaded silence had fallen over them. The air felt as if it was about to break.

Jack became fascinated with the ceiling, aiming his torch up there for long periods between brief glances at the uneven ground before him. In places it looked like a cave, with uneven rocky protrusions, stalactites made of some unidentifiable, creamy material, and dark cracks into which even his torch could not delve. Elsewhere he could see the rough concrete that sealed the canal beneath the ground. Perhaps it was an intentional covering-over, or maybe it had been hidden away bit by bit, buildings constructed to span and then smother the old waterway.

"Jack!" Sparky called. Jack paused and looked at where his friend was shining his torch. Just before Jack's feet was a hole in the canal's old bed, several feet wide and at least six deep. Its bottom was a mucky mess, the small pools of stagnant water reflecting only a sick, slick light back up at them. It stank. He'd almost walked into it.

"That would have been a good start," Jack muttered.

"You'd have smelled worse than usual, that's for sure." Sparky passed him by with a grin and stepped neatly around the hole.

Jack took more care after that. There was plenty to wonder at, but there was also his own safety to consider, and that had to come first. For two years he had been petrified about leaving Emily on her own. He'd had nightmares about drowning, feeling the darkness of deep water sucking him down, and all the while Emily was alone on a vast pebble beach far away, hands reaching in an impossible attempt to save him, her brother, until the last time he was pulled under, when he saw the shadows gathering at the beach's extremes . . . watching . . . waiting to make sure Jack was not about to surface again, before slicking across the beach towards his abandoned sister.

"You okay, Ems?" It was the name he'd used when she was very young, and she usually did not like hearing it. Their parents had used it all the time.

His sister glanced back and smiled, and he saw that she was more than okay. She was *enjoying* this. That bolstered his mood and drove away the memories of bad dreams, shadows fading on unknown pebbly beaches.

Lucy-Anne and Rosemary maintained the lead. Jack's girlfriend walked apart from the older woman, but Jack knew her well. She was trying to hide her fascination in case Rosemary saw it as a weakness. Lucy-Anne hated being beholden to anyone, and now they were all in the hands of this woman whom none of them knew.

They walked for half an hour. There was little chit-chat, but plenty of nervous energy. Jack wondered about Rosemary's friend Philippe, and how he saw routes and byways hidden to everyone else. What must that be like? How did he manage understanding such secrets? Jack found the world of the Irregulars both intriguing and disturbing, and whenever he tried to put himself in their place, he became afraid. His life had changed enough since Doomsday. He could only imagine what London's few, amazing survivors must have gone through.

The buried canal ended abruptly. Rosemary and Lucy-Anne came to a halt, standing side by side and shining their torches at a blank concrete wall. There was graffiti carved into the concrete, incongruous in such surroundings and more disquieting because of that. 'We've come heer to hyde.' The mis-spellings made the pronouncements even more otherworldly.

"Who wrote that?" Jenna asked.

"It looks very old," Rosemary said. "To be honest, it's the first time I've seen it. I came from the other way, remember?"

"So where *is* the other way?" Lucy-Anne asked, her question bearing a challenge. Jack thought she was getting nervous.

"Can't you see?" Rosemary said, a hint of humour in her voice that Jack didn't like. She was supposed to be leading them, not testing them. But then, she *was* from out of London. Perhaps being in a position of power was something she was not used to.

Jack and the others shone their torches around, looking for where their path might continue. The combined lights lit up the whole end of the tunnel, revealing little but wall, ground, concrete ceiling, and the old, crumbling tow paths on either side.

"No," Sparky said. "I don't see." He spun around and played his torch behind them, his action instantly making Jack nervous. *Trap?* he thought.

"Down there," Emily said. "Look! It looks like a wave of mud, but it's fresh." She aimed her torch at the base of the graffitied wall, revealing a drift of canal-bed mud resting against the concrete. It looked unremarkable to Jack; just another hump in the old canal's uneven floor.

"Good eyes," Rosemary said.

"SuperGirl," Emily said matter-of-factly, and everyone laughed.

Their spirits raised, the others stood back while Sparky and Emily scooped away handfuls of loose dirt, slowly revealing a dark opening at the base of the wall. It was small—barely large enough to crawl through—but Rosemary assured them it was the way to go.

"If I can do it at my age," she said, "all of us can."

"So you hid it on your way through?" Jack asked. "Buried it?"

"Yes. Ruined my nails." The old woman smiled, but in torch-light it looked grotesque.

"Why?"

Rosemary frowned, and Jenna and Lucy-Anne aimed their torches at her face. Jack held back a laugh; it was like an interrogation in some crappy movie.

Cringing against the light, Rosemary turned away. "It's a

secret," she said. "This way, this route, no one knows about it. No one but Philippe and me, and now you."

The torches lowered, giving light to Sparky and Emily once more.

"*Everything's* a secret," Rosemary continued. "We're going towards a place where secrets are currency, and survival means stealth. I never liked London before Doomsday, to tell the truth, but these days, I like it much less. It's as if in moving on, we've also regressed. Trust is a thing of the past."

"Tell me about it," Lucy-Anne said, and Rosemary looked at Jack's girlfriend, her eyes sad and heavy with the terrible things they had seen.

"We trust you," Jack said, surprising himself. Lucy-Anne glanced at him, eyebrows raised. "We do. We trust you. You lead us in, and we'll help however we can."

Rosemary smiled. "Thank you," she said. "All of you. But sometimes . . ." She drifted off and stared at the concrete wall.

"Sometimes what?" Sparky said, panting. He stood, face grimy and hands filthy from the dirt.

Rosemary sighed. "Sometimes, I think we've passed the point of no return."

Rosemary went first. Sparky offered, but she insisted, waving away objections and borrowing Sparky's torch. Maybe Jack's statement of trust had given her strength, or perhaps it made her want to prove herself more.

Lucy-Anne felt a begrudging admiration for the old woman. But trust? Not yet.

"Only a few feet," Rosemary said. They watched her crawl into the narrow crack at the base of the wall, pulling with her elbows and pushing with her booted feet, and the light she carried threw back curious shadows, as though there was something down there with her.

"I'm through," Rosemary called. Her voice was muffled, and came from miles away.

Sparky went next. In his enthusiasm he banged his head on the concrete, cursing and touching his scalp to check for blood. Lucy-Anne giggled, but only briefly, because no one accompanied her.

*Fair enough,* she thought. *Yeah, we all know how serious this is. Rosemary can stop the bleeding, but we're out of the world we know, now. We're facing danger and challenging it to bite back.*

Jenna went after Sparky, then Emily, pushing the camera bag before her.

"You okay?" Jack asked. They were alone here now, with only the muffled sound of their friends chatting with Rosemary. Lucy-Anne could not quite tell in what way their voices had changed.

"I'm fine. Just . . . you know."

"Bit scary, yeah?"

"I guess."

They stared at each other, knowing that perhaps now there should be a kiss or a hug, or at least something more than this.

"You next," she said, to break the silence more than anything. Jack smiled and nodded, reaching out towards her and barely managing to touch her hand with his.

She watched him crawl into the hole and, alone at last, she closed her eyes and gave way to a sob that had been building in her throat.

She could remember a dream she'd had weeks ago, when dogs were attacking her in the dark, biting her, eating her, even as she tried to fight them off. The body they'd seen . . . that had been like a trigger, throwing the dream back at her. She knew it was stupid. She knew they'd say she was a fool. But for a while back there, she'd been terrified.

At least now they were moving on.

She turned around slowly and shone the torch back the way they had come. Its beam did not reach very far. *Such old, thick darkness*, she thought, not sure where the idea came from. She suddenly felt like an invader down here.

The gap was much narrower than she'd expected, so much so that she could not even raise her head without bashing it as Sparky had done. So she stared at the gravelly ground beneath her, pushing with her feet and crawling through on her elbows. It was only as light fell upon her that she realised she was through.

Sparky helped her to stand, playfully brushing dust and dirt from her clothes. "Welcome to the Mines of Moria!" he said, in the gruffest voice he could manage.

Lucy-Anne looked around. "Bloody hell!"

"I think it's an old church basement," Rosemary said.

The room was twenty steps across and thirty long, supported at regular intervals by thick stone columns. There seemed to be nothing stored down here, and it had the feel of being long-abandoned; dust had drifted against the base of walls, and in one corner an impressive array of spider webs formed grubby curtains. They shone their torches around, searching but not finding a way up into whatever building had once stood, or still stood above them.

"Maybe over there," Jenna said. She walked toward one corner, kicking through the layered dust at her feet. She looked up at the ceiling, then back at the group, nodding. "Must have been closed in ages ago."

Lucy-Anne saw the discoloured ceiling above where Jenna stood. The evidence of a blocked in staircase, perhaps, or the remains of where a hatch had once led down to this place.

"Why'd you think it's a church?" Jack asked.

"Over there," Rosemary said. "In the end wall. That's the way we have to go. You'll see."

*We'll see what?* Lucy-Anne thought. She was about to ask when she heard the growl.

Her heart stuttered, missing a beat and taking her breath away when it restarted. Her arms and chest went cold. A sound returned from her dream, as fresh and alive as if she were dreaming it again now: another growl, and a low, throaty bark.

They were all frozen. The sudden stillness would have been comical, were it not for the other growls now answering the first.

"Oh, no," Rosemary groaned. And she sounded her age for the first time since Lucy-Anne had met her.

Emily dashed over to her brother's side. He glanced at Lucy-Anne, but she could not even blink.

"What?" Jack whispered. He stepped closer to Rosemary, and the others all turned to look at the old woman. Their eyes were wide in the darkness, glittering with strange yellow light. "Rosemary, *what?*"

"Dogs," Lucy-Anne whispered.

"Yes," Rosemary said. "I met them on the way out, but they were much further back, just beneath the Exclusion Zone."

"And?" Jack asked.

"They're wild, Jack. From London. There are packs in there, big packs."

"We've heard about them," Jenna said. All of them had drawn close, subconsciously shielding Emily from whatever danger approached.

"Some of them went down beneath the city," Rosemary said. "The Tube, tunnels, sewers. Dog, and . . ."

"Other things," Jenna finished for her.

Rosemary nodded. Lucy-Anne knew what "other things" meant, because they'd had a series of reports left in the drops close to Camp Truth a few months before. Much could be put down to hearsay and exaggeration, they'd agreed, but it also seemed likely that some of what they read was true. Alligators, snakes, poisonous frogs, deadly spiders, and even a pride of lions, all of them escaped from various zoos and private collections in and around London following Doomsday.

But dogs . . .

"I dreamed this," she whispered, and she was aware of Jack's torch shifting as he turned to look at her.

Another growl came, much closer than before, and there seemed to be cunning there, and purpose.

Jack stepped in front of Emily, a four inch folding knife in his hand. Jenna also shielded the girl, and Sparky already had a knife in each hand, torch tucked in his back pocket.

"How many were there?" Jack asked the old woman.

"Five," Lucy-Anne said.

"Yes," Rosemary said, surprised. "But I think I broke one of their legs."

"Four's still enough," Sparky said. "Shit. *Shit!* Why didn't you tell us?"

"Would you still have come?" Rosemary asked.

"Yes!" Sparky and Jack spoke at the same time, and the woman looked down at her feet.

*No*, Lucy-Anne thought, and when she blinked she saw a flash of her dream, a dog snarling with her own meat hanging from its teeth—

—and when she looked again, the growl was real.

The first dog emerged from the tunnel into the large basement, dodging their torch beams, darting from column to column as it came for them.

# CHAPTER SIX
# POINT OF NO RETURN

> News from London is contradictory and confusing. Official sources talk of at least nine separate terrorist attacks, including explosions at the London Eye, the Houses of Parliament, London Bridge, Leicester Square, and Buckingham Palace. A source at Scotland Yard has said that several terrorist cells are being actively pursued through London, and that more attacks are feared. There is still no clear news of which chemical or biological agent has been deployed. Eyewitness accounts tell of military roadblocks, bulldozers piling bodies in public parks, and execution-style shootings to contain certain areas of the population. Whatever is true, it's certain that this is a tragedy of extreme magnitude, and CNN will, of course, be broadcasting throughout the day to bring you updates as and when they become available.
>
> —*CNN: Tragedy in London, 12:42 p.m. EST, July 28, 2019*

Sparky crouched down low, a knife held in each hand, relying on the light from everyone else's torches to give him sight. Jack stood beside him to the left, but Sparky took a step forward, insisting that he be the first.

Jack had once seen his friend get into a fight with someone twice his age and a foot taller than him. The man had stormed in with fists waving and a shit-eating grin, catching Sparky one on the chin. Sparky had staggered back, ducked down, kicked him in the nuts, and when the guy fell over Sparky put the boot in. Thirty seconds later the man was out cold.

Sparky was not one to mess with, and he'd never been afraid of the sight of his own blood. Jack knew what Sparky's brother had become, and sometimes, like now, his friend actually scared him.

More shadows darted from the tunnel at the other end of the room. Torch lights flickered and bobbed after them, but the dogs possessed an almost supernatural ability to dodge into darkness.

The first hound emerged from behind a stone column and jumped at Sparky. Jack almost laughed: it was a King Charles Spaniel, its black and white coat smeared with mud, long ears flopping back as it leapt at his friend. But the laughter died in Jack's mouth when he saw the animal's teeth, its lips pulled back in a furious growl, and he realised how wild this dog had become. If anyone had ever stroked it with affection, the animal's memories of such moments were long forgotten.

Sparky stepped to the side and lashed out, but the dog snapped at his arm, catching his wrist with its sharp teeth. Sparky grunted and dropped a knife.

Jack took two steps and kicked the dog just as it landed on all fours. Distracted by the taste of Sparky's blood, it had not seen his foot coming, and his boot caught it beneath the jaw. Its head jerked up and back with a sickening *crunch* of teeth jamming shut.

Sparky knelt beside the dog and buried his remaining knife in its throat.

The animal squealed and howled, kicking its back legs, pinned to the ground by the blade. The sounds it made were piteous, and Jack glanced back at the others. He was pleased to see that Emily had her face buried in Jenna's shoulder.

"Look out!" Lucy-Anne shouted. She came toward him in a blur, and for a moment Jack was disorientated, his girlfriend's torch flashing across his eyes and blinding him to the shadows.

Something hit him in the hip. It was warm and wet, and he

realised that was a dog's nose nuzzling at the fat of his waist, and beneath that was the warmth of blood as its teeth broke his skin and it tried to burrow inside. *A dog is trying to eat me!* he thought, and the idea jarred him from wherever he'd been. He brought the torch down and smacked it against the dog's head. The animal whined and ran, leaving Jack's hip still feeling wet.

"Pitbull," Jenna said. "They were banned years ago."

"Someone forgot to tell that one," Lucy-Anne said. She was with him now, standing with her back to his so that together they could see all around. "Lucky. You must have caught it just right to drive it away, but it'll—"

"Lucky? My guts are pouring out and—"

"Don't be a wimp," she said, her voice high with panic. "Just a scratch. Sparky?"

Sparky stood from the dog now lying dead at his feet, wiping his knife quickly on its coat. His face looked grey, eyes deep and dark. His right hand and wrist were black with blood. "Yeah."

"Get your torch out," Lucy-Anne said.

"Yeah."

"Here they come!" Jenna shouted.

Light beams wavered and flashed, shadows danced, and within those shadows were the dogs. Jack could not count them, and in the chaos of the next couple of minutes he made no effort to do so. He simply fought. He kicked and punched, swung his torch, slashed out with his knife, edging close to Emily and keeping her at his back so that she was sandwiched between him and Jenna.

Rosemary seemed to drift in and out of the light, her arms and legs twisting and thrashing as she did her best to keep the dogs away from her flesh.

Jenna had started using her knapsack as a weapon, swinging it back and forth and—if a dog chose the moment between swings to come at her—kicking out with her heavy boots. Dogs yelped and growled, people roared and screamed, and Jack tried to stay focussed.

A flash of yellow to his left marked the third attack by a dog he thought was a Labrador, though it was ragged and thin. Its fur was streaked dark, its muzzle wet with blood. Jack hoped it was its own.

As the animal leaped, he ducked low and thrust up with the knife. The dog's paws scraped the side of his head and it howled. He felt a gush of warmth across his hand. Swinging his torch around, he was just in time to see the wounded animal dragging itself away between stone columns.

He looked around at the others. Sparky was fighting the pitbull, using his feet and knees to keep it away from him as he slashed out with his knife. His right hand was hanging by his side now, and blood had darkened his jeans. The dog was mad, foaming at the mouth, growling, scrabbling at Sparky's legs with its claws and gnashing its teeth. For every wound the boy put in its body, it gave him one back.

Behind Jack, Jenna still had Emily. His sister seemed unhurt, though she was looking around with unbridled terror. He hoped she did not try to run. Jenna hefted her backpack, caught Jack's eyes, smiled.

Lucy-Anne had picked up Sparky's dropped knife and was kneeling on the ground, stabbing repeatedly at a meaty mess that had once been a dog. For an instant Jack thought it was the King Charles Spaniel that Sparky had brought down, but then he saw that this animal was larger, its legs black and brown. She stabbed, slashed, hacked, and though the creature was obviously dead, her rage seemed to be growing.

"Jenna," Jack said, glancing back at his sister and friend.

Yet again, Jenna seemed to read his mind. She glanced past Jack at Lucy-Anne. "Go," she said. "I've got Emily."

Keeping an eye out for the injured Labrador, Jack hurried across to Lucy-Anne. As he drew close she span around and crouched, bloody knife in one hand, the other held out for balance. And for a moment shorter than a blink, he thought she was going to come at him. Her eyes were white pools in a face smeared with blood, her teeth bared, and she reminded him of one of their crazed attackers.

"It's dead," Jack said. A waving torch beam played across the corpse at Lucy-Anne's feet. Steam rose.

Lucy-Anne's eyes closed slightly, her lips softened over her teeth, and she stood.

"Watch out!" Emily called.

A yellow blur erupted from the shadows and struck Lucy-Anne from behind. She went down, eyes widening in surprise now rather than fury, and dropped Sparky's knife. Jack actually heard the wind knocked from her as she hit the ground, the Labrador falling on top of her.

He went to help, but not fast enough. The dog bit into the back of Lucy-Anne's neck, jaw working as it tried to penetrate skin, flesh and gristle. It shook its head, and as Jack thrust his knife between its ribs Lucy-Anne shrieked, a terrible sound that turned wet.

"Lucy-Anne!"

Sparky appeared by his side, kicking at the dog even as Jack stabbed it again. It died with a violent shudder. Sparky heaved it off, and Jack had to use his knife to prise its jaws apart, away from Lucy-Anne's neck. Someone kept their torch played on her, and Jack wished he could not see so much detail.

"The other one?" he asked.

"Dead," Sparky said. "All four, dead. Let's just hope there are no more."

"This is the same pack," Rosemary said.

Sparky surged upright, and from the corner of his eye Jack was aware of a flash of movement, a growl of anger. "You led us down into this!" Sparky said. He grabbed Rosemary by her coat's collar and almost lifted her, pushing her back against one of the stone columns. "We followed you down here, and all the time you knew what could be waiting for us!"

"I was afraid you wouldn't come!"

Lucy-Anne was moaning before him, Emily was crying, face pressed into Jenna's neck, and now Sparky was about to beat on the old woman. Jack knew they did not need this at all.

"Sparky!" he shouted. His friend turned. "I need you here. We're through it, but we're all hurt."

Sparky let go and came slowly to Jack's side. He was looking down at Lucy-Anne. There was so much blood.

"I'll help her first," Rosemary said. "Then you, Sparky. Then Jack. I think Jenna and Emily are unhurt, so—"

"You're not laying your pissing hands on me!" Sparky said. "No way! Bloody witch."

Lucy-Anne groaned again, trying to roll over onto her back. She raised one hand and clawed at Jack's boot, her fingers hooking into a lace. He felt her pull as she tried to sit up, but he leaned forward and eased her back down, whispering to her, telling her everything was going to be all right.

"She needs you now," he said, looking up at Rosemary.

The woman came. Jack backed away slightly, but he would not let go of Lucy-Anne's hand. He watched as Rosemary laid her hands on the girl's wounds, and he remembered the way it had felt when she had been healing the knife wound in his leg. There had been an intrusion there, an invasion of his flesh, but then he had passed out. Now, it was his turn to watch.

Rosemary healed Lucy-Anne's wounds from the inside out. Her hand seemed to enter the girl's torn neck, neither aggravating nor enlarging the existing wounds. Her fingers went deep. Then she slowly withdrew them, the tendons on the back of her hand flexing and stretching constantly, the fingers moving like individual living things as they emerged. By the time Rosemary had removed her hand fully, Lucy-Anne had stopped groaning.

The woman kept her fingertips in contact with the torn skin until it was healed over, and as she sat back with a sigh Jack leaned forward with his torch, searching for where the ugly bite marks had been, seeking the torn flesh, but finding smooth skin marred only by a smear of drying blood.

The others were silent. They had all been watching.

"That hand?" Rosemary said, nodding at Sparky's tattered right hand and wrist. The boy came forward, and Rosemary went to work again.

They waited in that subterranean room for an hour or more. Rosemary healed Sparky's hand and Jack's hip, and then she went back to Lucy-Anne and touched her more minor wounds. There were cuts and scrapes, bruises and bumps, and Rosemary's hands fixed them all.

Jack sat with Emily for a while, hugging her and talking with her. She no longer seemed to be afraid. He was once again stunned at how resilient his young sister was, and he wished he could live in the moment like her. The dead dogs disturbed her somewhat, but only because of the bloody meat of their injuries. The amazement at what Rosemary was doing seemed to wipe fear from the slate of her mind, and she watched wide-eyed as the woman touched cut skin and healed it without leaving a scar.

"It's just amazing," she said, over and over, and Jack could only agree. But he was still shaken by the attack. And however benevolent Rosemary's touch was now, he could not help wondering how much more she had decided to keep from them.

Jenna came and sat beside them, and she and Emily giggled over something Jack could not hear. The girls had always been close—Emily seemed to be the sister that Jenna had never had—and right now Jack was very grateful for that. He tried not to feel selfish, but sometimes he needed time. Sometimes, he needed to be on his own.

And other times, there were things he did not want Emily to hear.

"Alligators?" he said, kneeling beside Rosemary. The old woman had sat against one of the side walls, resting her head back against the stone and closing her eyes. She seemed tired. Jack did not care. "Snakes? A pride of lions? What more will we have to face before we get there?" He was speaking quietly, but he was aware of Sparky watching him from across the basement. They'd arranged two torches so that they gave much of the room a diffused, even light, and Sparky had taken it upon himself to collect the four dogs' corpses into one pile.

"Hopefully no more," the woman said. "Jack, listen to me. You're the leader of this little group, whether the others realise or acknowledge that, or not."

"We have no leader," he said.

"Not true. You know that. I think maybe it's because you have Emily, and you have to keep rooted. Have to stay strong."

"I'm looking after her."

"You *are*, son." Rosemary leaned close to him, becoming more animated. "And you're doing a fine job."

"I didn't come here for compliments," he said. "I came to ask you: Is there anything else you haven't told us?"

"About the tunnels, and the route to London? No. The dogs attacked me, I escaped, and the rest of my journey was uneventful. But about London itself? Yes, there's plenty I haven't told you. Some amazing things, and some horrible."

"Like the Nomad?" Jack asked, fishing for information. "We heard about that. A thing haunting London from before, untouchable and tortured. A legend, I suppose, but it sounded amazing *and* horrible."

"A legend?" Rosemary said, shrugging and glancing aside. "Perhaps. London is full of them, now. There's so much you'll have to find out for yourself."

Jack looked across to Emily and Jenna, then at Sparky dragging the last dog's corpse across the ground. Lucy-Anne sat against a stone pillar, looking at the knife Sparky had let her keep, its reflection travelling the room as she turned it slowly in her hand. He considered what Rosemary had said, and nodded.

"That'll do for now," he said. "But you know the trust is damaged, don't you?"

"I know. And I wish I could do something to repair it."

"Tell us the truth from now on," Jack said, standing. "That'll do, for a start." He walked away, but paused a few steps from Rosemary. He turned around and patted his hip where the dog had chewed into him. "Rosemary. Thanks for . . ."

The old woman nodded and smiled.

On their way into the tunnel from which the dogs had emerged, Rosemary pointed out the evidence that this basement had once been below a church. In the corner beside the tunnel mouth stood a font, its water bowl cracked and covered in moss. The little water that stood in there was so black that it could have been blood.

"I wonder if the church is still up there?" Jenna said, looking up at the ceiling. "And if it is, maybe someone's in there right now."

"We're in a different place now," Lucy-Anne said, her voice was low and quiet. She felt haunted. She wondered just how close she'd come to dying, and she thought about asking Rosemary the next time they had a quiet moment. But on the other hand, she wasn't sure she really wanted to know.

*It wasn't* exactly *the same*, she kept thinking. But dream memories are deceitful things, and the more she thought about it, the more reality and dream had begun to merge.

"This tunnel's another reason I think this was a church," Rosemary said. "It's long, and there are a few places where it used to branch off. I think it might have been an escape tunnel between churches hundreds of years ago."

"Escape from what?" Emily asked.

"Persecution," Jenna said. "People of one religion not liking people of another. Hunting them. Sometimes killing them."

Emily snorted. "That's just *stupid*."

They left the basement room splashed with droplets of their own blood and the promise of rot. Sparky and Rosemary went first this time, Lucy-Anne walking on her own behind them, the others following her. Jack approached her a couple of times, but she gave him a distant smile and shook her head. *Not yet*, she thought. *I need to get things square in my own mind first*.

As she walked, she tried to remember the other strange dreams and nightmares she'd been having. But though she knew they were there, they kept themselves hidden well away.

*Underground for a couple of hours, and already we've all nearly died*, Jack thought. The tunnel was so narrow that in some places they had to go in single file. In these places Rosemary insisted on going first, perhaps some small penance for what they had been through.

Emily walked just ahead of him, filming again. He could see the viewing screen of her camera, and noticed that much of the time it was focussed on Lucy-Anne's back. *Good*, he thought. *My little sis knows where the mystery is*.

"So who do you think left the picture of your mother?" Jenna asked quietly. She was walking at their rear. Jack glanced back at her and shrugged.

"At first, I thought it was obvious. Her. Rosemary. But now I'm not so sure. She swore she didn't put the pictures there, and why would she lie if she did? We'd already committed to coming in with her. We'd have committed to it even if she told us about the dogs."

"She was just being cautious," Jenna said. "I guess there was always a chance we'd never meet them."

"A chance, yeah."

Emily must have heard them chatting, because she turned and walked backward for a while, training her torch and the camera lens on them. Jack gave her a thumbs-up, and Jenna laughed and waved.

"The intrepid explorers venture deeper into unknown territory . . ." Emily whispered into the microphone, hurrying on ahead until she walked beside Sparky. He gave her a goofy grin and started making faces at the camera, obviously enjoying the attention.

"So if it wasn't Rosemary, then who?" Jenna asked. "Bit of a coincidence."

"A lot of one," Jack agreed. The tunnel was wider here, and he and Jenna started walking side by side. It was easier to talk that way, and he enjoyed making eye contact with her. She was a good friend. "I dunno, I feel a bit . . ."

"I know," Jenna said. "You know your mum's alive, but Sparky and Lucy-Anne are walking into the dark."

"That's one way of putting it." Jack smiled and reached out, squeezing Jenna's shoulder. She surprised him by leaning in quickly and giving him a strong hug, then going on ahead.

"Your turn to bring up the rear," she said. "The quiet we've left behind gets heavy after a while."

"I've got big shoulders."

They went on, and Jack discovered that Jenna was right. Before him was subdued chatter, the sound of shoes scraping the floor and clothes brushing against the walls. Behind him . . . nothing but darkness and silence. They both took on weight very quickly.

He thought a little about what Lucy-Anne had said before the dogs attacked, about dreaming it. Strange, but she was a strange girl. Back when they'd still been sleeping together, she'd frequently woken up with a start, always claiming to not remember the nightmares that had woken her. She'd suffered more than all of them, he supposed, being left on her own in that big, empty house. She must have a head full of nightmares.

The tunnel ended in another room, smaller than the basement where the dogs had attacked. From here Rosemary led them through a series of small chambers and connecting tunnels, and here and there they passed through tumbled walls, crawling and squirming their way through narrow gaps. Beyond, they entered a place that kept its origins a mystery: tunnel or cave? It was difficult to decide, and Jack spent half an hour trying to make out which was the case. The place had an uneven floor and fissures across its walls and ceiling, but here and there he was sure he could make out tool marks.

Sparky's shout startled him from his contemplation.

"Hey, you lot! I'm bloody starving! Rosemary says there's a place up ahead where we can stop for lunch."

At the mention of food, Jack's stomach rumbled. The fact that he was still hungry after what they had been through, he saw as a good sign. *Need to go moment by moment*, he thought. *The past has gone. The future is waiting. It's the here and now that matters most.*

They found somewhere beautiful. It was so unexpected that Jack had to blink several times to make sure everything was real. They climbed some stone steps and emerged inside a ruined church, its walls blackened by an old fire, charred ceiling timbers littering the floor, windows long-since vanished and steeple tumbled down. But the walls were still solid, and because the roof had gone, the insides were a riot of wild undergrowth, unchecked for many years. A thick, heavy curtain of clematis covered two walls, smothering window openings and bursting with pink and yellow flowers. Another wall hung with wisteria, swinging with pendulous sprays of mauve blooms, and the final wall, below which the remains of what may have been an altar lay in ruins, was home to a gorgeous, heavily thorned yellow rose. The floor of the church was awash with colour and a low, tangled plant that Jack could not identify.

"Wow," Jenna said. Nobody else could think of anything more suitable, so they stared around in silence.

"Sorry," Rosemary said. "I forgot to tell you about this place, as well."

Jack smiled. And then Emily was running, dashing here and there, filming, lifting shrub branches and delving beneath, and a robin landed on a bush close to where they all stood.

"Seems quite tame," Lucy-Anne said. "How close are we to people in here?"

"We're right on the edge of the Exclusion Zone." Rosemary spoke quietly, as though to mention those words could spoil this place.

"This has been ruined for more than two years, though," Sparky said.

Rosemary shrugged. "I assume so. Just another part of the route that Philippe gave me."

"So where to from here?" Jack asked.

"A dangerous part," the woman said. "The riskiest when it comes to being seen. A dash across the old churchyard, then over a narrow road that used to lead to a housing estate. It leads nowhere now, but it's still close to the Exclusion Zone, and there may be military patrols."

"After that?" Lucy-Anne asked.

"Down again. A dried-up stream that leads to an old sewage treatment works. A tunnel. Then under the Exclusion Zone, and we'll be in London."

"We're that close?" Sparky said.

Rosemary nodded at the clematis-covered wall. "It looks like a clear day. Take a look."

Sparky glanced at Jack, frowning, but Emily had been listening and she was there before all of them. She snuggled herself through the trailing clematis plant, pushing through with the camera, and then they all heard her intake of breath. Jack did not realise just how much she had been nattering commentary at the camera until she stopped.

"Emily?" he said.

"It's all gone." Her voice was very small, and very vulnerable.

Sparky and Lucy-Anne pulled aside the hanging plants, and the four of them pushed their way through, standing beside Emily by one of the empty window openings.

They had all heard many stories of the Exclusion Zone, read plenty of eyewitness accounts of what it looked like, and over the past two years there had been at least a dozen drops of photographs of this place close to Camp Truth. But some things simply had to be seen.

Jack could barely believe that such talent for destruction could exist in humankind.

There were buildings around the church—houses, shops, and the blocky outline of an old school. They all seemed to be abandoned. Beyond them, to the east, was a place where similar buildings had once stood. Now, there was only ruin. No wall had been left standing, and the piles of rubble, some higher than Jack's head, disappeared into the distance. They reminded him of scenes he'd seen of the Sahara, only these dunes were of brick, slate, and stone, rather than sand. Many areas had been scoured by fire, scars on the grey landscape that had reduced the rubble to dull black boils. A few tree stumps were visible, but even these had been bulldozed down or destroyed in explosions.

Here was the Exclusion Zone, created by the Choppers to protect the rest of Britain from what had happened in London. Here was the terrible evidence of the government's scorched earth policy, an attempt to create an unbreachable cordon across which no one could go, and nothing could come. Here was destruction, and beyond, perhaps two miles distant, Jack could see a line of buildings standing in the hazy summer heat.

There was London. There was the Toxic City. And somewhere beyond the boundary of those buildings—maybe even in one of those he was looking at right now—his mother, and perhaps his father.

"We're so bloody close," Sparky said.

"What have they done?" Lucy-Anne whispered, her voice broken, face wet with tears. Jack touched her, and she fell shivering into his embrace. He felt the wetness of her tears against his shoulder, and his own eyes blurred.

"There's no going back now," Jenna said.

"This sight is something many of you may have imagined, but never seen," Emily said, slowly panning the camera across the staggering ruins. "But viewers, beyond this image is a lie about to be uncovered. Prepare yourselves. Soon, you will witness the truth of the Toxic City."

# CHAPTER SEVEN
# THE END OF BEAUTY

> The culprits for these cowardly acts are still at large. All Londoners should remain at home and await further instructions. Do not attempt to flee the city. Do not attempt travel of any kind. Further attacks are expected. The prime minister will be giving a live statement on all TV and radio channels at 7:00 p.m.
>
> —*Government Statement, all-channel broadcast,*
> *6:15 p.m. GMT, July 28, 2019*

They lowered the clematis back across the window and ate the food they had brought. The church was still a beautiful place, but the air was marred by the knowledge of what lay beyond. Once they left here, Jack suspected they would be leaving that beauty behind.

The robin returned to watch them eat. Sparky threw a bread crust its way, but it hopped back and ignored the offered food. Jenna crumbled the crust from a jam tart and sprinkled it across the undergrowth. The bird watched her, head jerking this way and that as though expecting ambush at any minute.

Emily crawled forward with the crusts from her own sandwich. She broke them into many pieces, then held out her hand as far as she could stretch.

"Not a chance," Lucy-Anne said, but she grew still as they watched the little bird. It hopped from the wisteria and came close, eyeing them all suspiciously, but was apparently unconcerned at Emily's presence.

Jack saw that she held the camera in her other hand, the lens trained on her hand offering the crumbs.

The bird hopped closer, hesitated, then jumped into Emily's palm.

Jack heard her intake of breath. He wished he could see her face.

Eventually the bird hopped away, and their small group was taken with a flutter of excitement. They finished their food and passed a water bottle around, all of them aware that every mouthful and swallow brought them closer to leaving this place.

"I never liked London," Sparky said. "Shit-hole. Bloody place made my brother what he was." He toyed with a long leafy plant stem, winding it around his finger. "What he *is*."

Jack was surprised. Sparky rarely talked about Stephen, and certainly not to an audience. Sometimes, after a few ciders, the two of them would discuss him for a while, but it always ended up with Sparky getting angry, his voice turning hard and exuding violence. Jack had always thought that talking, *really* talking, was just what he needed.

"How?" Jenna asked, and Jack could have kissed her.

"Went there to join a band," Sparky said. "Mum and Dad didn't want him to go, said he should stay on in school and go to university. More they said that, the more determined he became." He laughed. "Band was called *Deep Shit*. Steve liked that, said that when they made it big he could always answer people asking what he did by saying, 'I'm in *Deep Shit.*' Well, he soon was." He drifted off, concentrating far too hard on the plant stem. Jack noticed his friend's face flushing.

"What sort of band was it?" Jenna asked.

"Punk. Real punk, not the pop sort that was popular a few years back. Music with bollocks. But the singer, Charlie, was a waster. He wasn't really there for the music, not like Steve. He thought they'd make it big, make loads of money, do what they want. Thing is, he spent it before they made it. Booze and drugs, and girls attracted by the glamour of it all." Sparky shook his head, as though amazed for the first time at what had happened to his brother.

"It's strange what some people see as glamorous," Rosemary said. Sparky glanced up, and for a moment Jack thought he was going to shout her down. But then he nodded.

"Yeah. Steve never did, not really. But being aware of how crap all that stuff was . . . it didn't help him. Mum and Dad blame him completely, but I blame *them*. Never let him do anything he wanted. Kept him at home, trying to protect him they said, because they had this thing about how big and nasty the world was. They knew it was, 'cos they saw it all on telly, read it in the papers. Huh."

They waited quietly, letting Sparky take his time. Even Emily was silent, leaning against Jack as if for protection from where this story was going.

"So he rebelled," Sparky continued. "What a bloody cliché, eh? He took the drugs to get back at Mum and Dad. Least, that's what I think. They just blamed him, disowned him, never took his calls. And he stayed there in London when the band fell apart before it had really begun, and . . ." He started crying.

"I think we all know the story from there," Rosemary said after a while, and Jack winced and closed his eyes, because now surely Sparky's fury would fly.

But sometimes grief can overcome fury, and smother it. "That's just it," Sparky said, his voice sad and lost. "None of us knows, not really. We know what happened to London. But something like that . . . it's not one story, it's a million. That's why I want to find him. *Need* to find him. To hear *his* side of the story." He lowered his head again and wiped at his eyes, unashamed in his sadness.

After a minute or two Jenna stood and went to him. She sat by his side, not touching him, silent, but Jack could see that her simply being there meant the world.

Jack and Emily went first. The churchyard was even more overgrown than the ruined building itself, and it was impossible to hurry without risking a fall. There were still gravestones showing their humped grey shoulders above the undergrowth, and hidden beneath would be tomb slabs and other promises of broken bones. But the lushness also provided good cover, and they crawled their way towards the church's boundary.

*Over the road, into the ditch, right, and then left*. It sounded so easy. But Rosemary's directions could not convey distance, nor the fact that there were great swathes of vicious stinging nettles all across the churchyard.

They moved slowly, carefully, doing their best to avoid the nettles and always listening for noises that may warn of danger. In the distance Jack could hear motors, so faint that there was no way of telling whether or not they were approaching. Closer, there was only the singing of birds, and the soft, secret whispers of plants moving in a warm summer breeze.

When they reached the edge of the churchyard, they followed the boundary wall until they found a grilled gate. The hinges looked rusted, but there was no lock or chain, and Rosemary had told him that she'd come this way.

"Ready?" Jack asked.

Emily nodded, rubbing at a rash of stings across one forearm. "Need some dock leaves."

Jack smiled. "Mum always told us that, didn't she?" Emily tried to smile back.

Jack leaned against the gate and looked back along the road. Nothing. Then he turned and looked toward the Exclusion Zone. He could see where the road finished in a pile of rubble, the tarmac crushed and cracked by whatever heavy vehicle had been used to demolish so many buildings. Again, nothing. They seemed to be completely alone.

The Exclusion Zone spooked him. So many people had lived there, and now they were gone, along with all trace of their existence. A place that had once been so full of life was now barren and sterile. The breeze lifted drifts of dust-clouds across the broken landscape, and he could imagine they were something else.

"I'll go first," Jack whispered. "If you hear or see anything wrong, go straight back to the church."

"And leave you?" Emily's eyes went wide, the mere thought of being parted from her brother patently terrifying.

Jack touched her shoulder and squeezed. "Don't worry," he said. He could think of nothing else to say. "I'll go first." This was so dangerous that if he *was* seen, there would be no easy way out for any of them.

*Cameras?* he thought. *Microphones, satellite surveillance, dogs? They wouldn't leave the Exclusion Zone unwatched or unprotected, surely?* But Rosemary had come this way, and that was all he could hold on to.

He gave Emily a quick kiss on the cheek, pulled the gate open and ran. His feet kicked up dust from the road, grinding in the grit on its surface. It was only two lanes wide, but it seemed to take forever to reach the other side and fall into the ditch.

The ditch was filled with nettles as well. Jack gasped as they touched him across one arm and beneath his chin, raising sore welts that would take hours to fade away. He squatted, turned, and looked back at the church. Nobody shouted, nobody came, no vehicles sprang to life. He could almost believe that he had made it.

Cautiously, he lifted his head above the edge of the ditch and looked across at the gate. Emily was there, staring right back at him.

He gave a thumbs-up and she smiled, returning the gesture. Then she slipped through the gate and followed his route across the road.

"Careful!" he whispered as she dropped in beside him. "More nettles!"

"I'm okay." She had her camera out again, Jack noticed, and she poked it over the ditch to get a shot of the church.

"Come on, the others will follow soon. We need to get back under cover."

"I like feeling the sun."

"Me too," Jack said. But after only three or four hours underground, up here he felt so exposed.

They moved slowly along the ditch bottom, doing their best to dodge the worst of the nettles, stomping on those they could not bypass. When a telegraph pole cast its shadow across the ditch Jack looked up, expecting to see a camera fixed to its side and swivelling to follow their progress. But all it held were two limp cables, long since cut.

The ditch branched left and they went that way, following Rosemary's directions. A shopping trolley blocked their path, and Jack felt a weird rush of nostalgia for something so innocuous. Years ago, before Doomsday, some kids had probably swiped this trolley and used it for a bit of fun: rides along the road; jumping hastily erected timber ramps. Then they'd dumped it, and it had been here ever since, rusting into the landscape as the world changed around it. He wondered where those kids were now, and whether they still had fun.

He climbed around the trolley and helped Emily, then they went on until the ditch ended with a narrow culvert, much too small for them to enter. Jack paused, frowning, and looked back the way they had come.

"We came the right way," he said. "I'm sure."

"Here," Emily said. "Is this what she meant?" She was looking over the top of the culvert, filming across ground level at whatever lay beyond. Jack stood beside her.

The large area before them held several ground-tanks, all of them covered with heavy metal covers. Pipes and frames hung over them, many bent and twisted by some unknown force, and rust stained much of the metal.

"Sewage treatment plant," Jack said.

"Oh, great. That's going to smell just lovely." Emily panned the camera around and lowered it, dropping back down to sit in the ditch.

"It's dry down here," Jack said, joining her. "And I doubt this has been treating anything for a couple of years."

Emily looked up sharply, lifting a finger to her lips.

Jack looked back along the ditch, and moments later he saw the shapes coming towards them. Sparky first, bent over so that he could not be seen above ground level. Jenna followed him, and behind her came Rosemary and Lucy-Anne, Jack's girlfriend keeping close to the older woman.

"I don't think there's anyone around," Sparky said when he reached them. "If we were seen, they'd have come for us by now."

Jack could not help recalling some of the stories from the drops close to Camp Truth—kidnappings, disappearances, executions. And he could see in Jenna's haunted eyes that she was thinking the same. Her father had been taken, and returned, but now he was a different man. A *lesser* man. Capture would mean the end for all of them, whether that end was death or something else.

"You need to lead us from here," he said to Rosemary.

"It's not far," she said, gasping for breath. "We'll be out of the sun again in a minute."

"And next time we see it we'll be in the Toxic City," Lucy-Anne said. Her eyes were hard, and when she glanced at Jack he sensed a shocking distance already growing between them.

"We still like to call it London," Rosemary said. "It hasn't been toxic for a long time."

Lucy-Anne nodded, still looking at Jack. *What?* he wanted to say. *What is it?* But he had never really understood her.

Sparky stood, looked around for a long time, then nodded. Rosemary climbed from the ditch and hurried across an area of long grass until she stood on concrete paving between metal tank covers. The others followed.

Beside the closest tank cover, there was a small hatch in the ground. The cover was metal as well, but light. Rosemary took a hooked metal manhole key from her pocket, curved it into a recessed ring in the cover and swung it upward. As she started down the small concrete staircase revealed beneath, she glanced up at the others. Her face softened, and for the first time Jack wondered whether she was a mother, and if so, where her husband and children were right now. He felt terrible for not asking, but now it seemed too late.

"It's not far now," Rosemary said.

"Back down into the dark again," Lucy-Anne said. There was something in her voice Jack had never heard before. He thought maybe it was fear.

"Yes, dear, but not for long. We're almost there."

"If there's anything else you need to warn us about—" Jack began.

"The dogs are dead," Rosemary said. "You killed them, together. I can't pretend the city isn't dangerous, but then you all know that, don't you?"

Emily separated from the small group and trained her camera on them. "The final descent before we rise into the Toxic City," she said. "And then we'll go to find who we came for." Even keeping the camera before her eye could not hide the tear that streaked her cheek.

"I'm not afraid," Lucy-Anne said. But as she followed Rosemary down, every jerky, determined movement she made was testament to her lie.

Lucy-Anne was afraid of her nightmares.

The dogs from her dream had come and bitten her, and after everyone had set off from the ruined church, and it was only her and Rosemary left, she'd asked the old woman how close she had been to death. *Its teeth nipped your spine*, Rosemary had said, *but I touched it and made it better*.

*How close?* Lucy-Anne had demanded.

*Very*, Rosemary had said, before rushing across the road into the ditch.

Now, descending back into the darkness once again, Lucy-Anne waited for other nightmares to make themselves known. She refused to believe it had been coincidence, because after what she'd been through that would be too cruel.

But if not coincidence . . . what?

*Have I had nightmares about falling?* she wondered, and her feet reached the foot of the ladder. *Rats carrying plague?* But there were no vermin that she could see down here. *My friends, killing me?* She looked around at the others, and she suddenly wanted to fold up and cry out at the betrayal her imagination was capable of.

"Nearly there, everyone!" she said, amazing even herself with her upbeat voice. "We've been waiting for so long, and now we're almost there!"

Smiles were exchanged, and they went on their way.

To begin with, their path was simple. After descending the concrete steps they found themselves in a long tunnel that ran the length of the sewage treatment works, with shorter tunnels projecting off at right angles. The smell was subtle and subdued—much to Emily's obvious relief—and just before they reached the end, Rosemary opened a metal hatch in the wall. They took it in turns, squeezing through, shining their torches on the opening and into the tunnel revealed beyond. This one had a low ceiling that meant they all had to crouch down, and cockroaches scuttled away from their torch light.

This tunnel ended with a blank wall, but an opening had been smashed through, revealing an uneven, sloping route that led deeper. They followed Rosemary, emerging into a large, brick-lined chamber that seemed much older that the treatment plant built just beside it. It was the converging point of four large sewage pipes. This place *did* stink, even though none of the pipes seemed to be carrying very much. One of them trickled a small, steady flow of dirty water into the chamber, but the other three appeared dry.

"Oh, that's pleasant," Sparky said. "Reminds me of Lucy-Anne's armpits."

Lucy-Anne did not reply. Sparky looked at her and she raised an eyebrow, and that was enough to make him smile.

"Rats everywhere," Jenna said. They did not seem to bother her, but Emily remained close to Jack, even while she trained her torch around the walls and filmed what it revealed.

"You'll see a lot more," Rosemary. "But there's always a balance. Lots of wild cats in London now, and they keep the rat population down."

She headed off, confidently aiming for one of the large sewage pipes.

"We walk through there?" Lucy-Anne asked. She hated this; she had never been afraid before. She could not prevent herself from shaking, and she'd seen the way Jack had been looking at her: concerned and confused.

"Not for long."

The pipe swept this way and that, branching left and right, but Rosemary did not hesitate at all. She took one branch that narrowed considerably, but they were happier to bend almost double, accepting the burning pain in their knees and back, rather than crawl. There was dried stuff here, sewage and dead rats and other things they could not so easily identify.

And at last Lucy-Anne found something to cling onto and calm her, and that was the memory of her family. Their smiles and voices drove away the threat of forgotten nightmares. Whatever happened in the near future, she was determined of one thing: she would discover the truth.

That's what drove them all, she was sure. Not the sense of injustice, and the knowledge that the government had lied to them day in, day out, since Doomsday. It was family that made them able to do this. Jack's and Emily's parents, and Sparky's brother. Even Jenna, who had lost no one on Doomsday, was coming here to avenge what they had done to her father since then.

She felt a momentary flush of hope and determination, and pride in her friends. If they weren't half-crawling through a pipe coated with dried shit and dead rats, she'd have hugged them all.

She could imagine Sparky's reaction to that.

Lucy-Anne giggled. She tried to stop, but couldn't. Her torch light shook as she laughed, and they all paused because they thought something was wrong.

"No!" she said, shaking her head even though none of them could see much down here. "No, it's okay, its . . ." Her laughter turned manic.

"Gas down here sometimes," Rosemary said, her voice low with concern.

"Nobody strike a match," Sparky said, and that only made Lucy-Anne laugh louder.

The sewers ended in another large chamber, and in this one they found a dead body.

It was a woman, sitting back against the wall, long hair tangled across her face and down one side of her head. She wore jeans and a heavy ski jacket, and rats had eaten her eyes.

That's what Jack noticed first, and what he could not help looking at again and again. He jerked his torch back at her face, knowing he should not, knowing that he should be turning the other way and leading Emily across the chamber and into whichever sewer they had to walk along next . . . and *rats had eaten her eyes*!

"Oh," Lucy-Anne said, backing away against the wall of the chamber. But she kept her eyes open.

"Rosemary—" Jack began, but she cut in.

"Not when I came through!" she said. "She wasn't here when I came through."

"You know her?" Jenna asked.

Rosemary went closer, stepping carefully across the lower part of the chamber, dodging still-wet pools of raw sewage.

"Jack . . ." Emily said. She lowered the camera. "I don't think I want to film this."

Jenna was with them then, holding Emily's hand and turning around so that they both faced away from the body.

"No," Rosemary said. She had lifted the woman's hair from her face and stepped aside, allowing torchlight to fall there. "I don't know her."

"Then what the hell is she doing down here?" Sparky said. "You said you're the only one who knew this route, you said that Philippe bloke told you the way, and—"

"Lots of Irregulars come down below London," Rosemary said. She turned her back on the body, hiding it from view. "To escape, to hide. There are some that can't handle what's happened to them, and . . ." She shrugged.

"She killed herself?" Jack asked.

"Maybe." Rosemary returned to them, leaving the dead woman behind. "Or maybe she was dying anyway, and she wanted to do it alone."

"We're still under the Exclusion Zone, right?" Jenna asked.

Rosemary thought about that for a while, then nodded. "Just. But soon, we enter an old Tube station that has been abandoned for years, walk along the line, and then we're there."

"So there'll be others?" Jack asked. "More people below ground?"

"There are plenty. But I doubt we'll see them. As I said, most of them come down here to be alone."

There was a heavy torch by the dead woman's left hand, and to her right an empty whiskey bottle lay on its side, a plastic bowl upended beside that. Last meal and drink.

"I wonder what she could do," Rosemary mused.

"That's someone's mother," Jenna said, angry. "Someone's sister."

"We should go," Jack said. "I don't want to stay down here anymore. Rosemary, I just want to get there and see the sun again. How far?"

"An hour."

"An hour." Lucy-Anne was staring at the woman, torch playing unwaveringly on her mutilated face.

"Lucy-Anne," Jack said. "Come on." He stepped before her, blocking her view and wanting so much to reach out and hold her. But the distance was still there, and he didn't think he had arms long enough.

The sewer ended in a place of chaos. The pipe had ruptured and smashed, and the solid ground around it had apparently been washed away by some vast underground flood. The void left behind looked precarious and in danger of collapse at any moment. Roots hung dead and shrivelled from the ceiling, and the fractured ends of underground pipes and ducting protruded like broken bones. Rosemary led them across, stepping around and over rocks and cracks in the ground, towards a small crawlspace at the other side.

"This is narrow," she said, facing the group of friends. "But not very long. And on the other side, there's the abandoned Tube station."

"Are we under London yet?" Jenna asked.

"Almost," Rosemary said. She looked up at the roof and the others shone their torches there, as though they could see all the way through. "Very close now. This is part of what they did to the Exclusion Zone, part of the damage." She shook her head, and just before she turned away, Jack thought he saw tears.

She was right, the crawlspace was very narrow. But they pulled their way through, lured by the promise of an easy walk and the end of the beginning of their quest.

Jack and the others had seen a few grainy images of London's Tube network since Doomsday, smuggled out with other pictures on memory cards tied to pigeons' legs or dogs' collars. They usually showed stations they were familiar with, only a little run down; litter on the platform, dust thick on the tiles, the spaces illuminated by heavy torches or small fires. But the place they found when they emerged from the crack in the earth was very different.

"Where the hell are we?" Sparky asked.

Jenna laughed. "I think it must be Christmas!"

The meagre light from their torches reflected from dozens of mirrors arrayed along the platform and down on the line, glitter balls hanging from the ceiling and smashed glass swept in drifts against the platform wall to their left, flooding the station with light. Swathes of bunting zig-zagged back and forth just above head height for the full length of the platform. In many places, tiles had fallen or been smashed from the wall, but the blank gaps left behind had been painted with luminous green, yellow, or blue paint. Halfway along the platform, there was even a crazy tree made from heavy wire, pinned with hundreds of small passport-sized photographs. Jack went to the tree and saw that each photo was of a different person. Some smiled, some frowned, some stuck out their tongues.

But among this colour and the enthusiastic splash of light, there was no sign of recent human habitation. Plenty of rats, true. And Jack saw footprints—a dog's? A wolf's?—which he was sure were trodden in dried blood.

"This station's been out of use for almost twenty years," Rosemary said. "Really was the end of the line! So those who lived underground—and there's always been a lot of them—adopted it as their own. Decorated it, slept here, used it as a retreat from above. The stairs are blocked off, and I suppose there must have been other ways up and down, but they've long gone."

"Where are they now?" Jack asked. "If they were . . . you know . . . moved from society anyway, how come they're not still here?"

"Doomsday touched everyone," Rosemary said, "and Evolve seeped everywhere. There are places in London that are graves. Huge graves. You'll see one soon, but . . . there's no way I can really prepare you for it." She looked around the group, and her expression truly startled Jack for the first time. She was an old woman, with the eyes of someone who had known far too much sadness, but she looked at them as though she were sorry for them all.

"It's sad," Lucy-Anne said.

"'Course it is," Sparky said. "Life's sad, and shit."

"No, no," Jack's girlfriend said. "This place. Even those who wanted nothing to do with the outside world were affected. Don't you see?"

"I see," Jack said, and he meant it. Lucy-Anne looked at him, and he felt included in her thoughts for the first time since they'd left Camp Truth.

"Well, I want to leave," said Emily. She had filmed the station, but the red light on her camera was no longer blinking. "Feels weird down here. Haunted."

None of them disputed her choice of words.

They walked along the old underground line, constantly aware of the flicker of movement just beyond the influence of their artificial light; rats, moving away, but not too fast. Jack guessed they'd had a fine feeding season a couple of years before, and maybe these descendants of those fattened things remembered the taste of human meat.

When they reached the next station it was grim and drab, and half of a train carriage protruded from the tunnel at its far end. The station name had been torn from the wall and smashed from the tiles, as though identity had no place in this new world.

"From here, we go up," Rosemary said.

"About bloody time," Sparky said.

None of them stopped walking, because they were all ready to see sunlight once more. But the mood between them was tense . . . and excited.

Here was the Toxic City.

Here was London.

# CHAPTER EIGHT
# FERTILE GROUND

> There will be a statement from the prime minister on all TV and radio channels at 8:00 p.m.
>
> —*Government Statement, all-channel broadcast, 7:08 p.m. GMT, July 28, 2019*

Jack felt the heat of the setting sun before he saw it. Soon it would be dusk, but the afternoon warmth felt very good as they climbed up from the Underground and stood at the crossroads of two London streets.

At first glance it could have been a quiet Sunday morning. Cars were parked along the roadside, if a little haphazardly in places, and a few shops had their front doors propped open. Pigeons cooed quietly on window sills. Litter whispered along the street, blown by a gentle breeze. But there was no life here, no breath, no heartbeat. This was obviously a dead place, and with that realisation came the facility to see evidence of that demise.

One of the propped-open doors rested against a skeleton in a dark blue uniform. Several shops' windows were smashed. Along the street, almost hidden behind an incongruous growth of brambles and rose bushes, a burnt-out pub poked charred rafters at the sky.

"It looks . . ." Lucy-Anne began. Jack could see her eyes flitting across the scene, going from windows to doors, cars to side-streets. *Is she looking already?* he thought, but he did not have to ask. Although he knew the size of London, he felt closer to his mother and father than he had in a long time.

"We have to be careful," Rosemary said, urging them back into the shadow of the Tube station entrance. "Choppers patrol the streets around this time of day. They don't like the dark, but they roam the dusk, when Irregulars are looking for somewhere to spend the night."

"You don't have somewhere permanent to live?" Jenna asked.

"Some do," Rosemary said. "But not many. Far too dangerous."

She looked terrified, and Jack could not detect a shred of pleasure in her at being back in London. Rather than coming home, Rosemary seemed to have brought herself back to danger.

"So where do *we* spend the night?" Sparky asked. "I've had enough of tunnels and rats."

"There's somewhere I know," Rosemary replied. "North, across the Barrens."

"Barrens?" Jack asked.

"The grave I told you about," the woman said. "You'll see. Not far from here. You'll see." She looked around the group, nodded, and then stepped out onto the pavement.

They followed her in line, Emily holding the camera before her and sweeping it slowly around. The station stood on one corner of a crossroads, and Rosemary led them around the side of the building, past peeling posters advertising movies and stage shows two years and many lifetimes old.

"Will we see lots of people?" Emily asked.

"Not around here," Rosemary said. "Not this close."

"Close to the Barrens?" Jack asked. But Rosemary only glanced back at him with haunted eyes.

Around the next corner they turned left into a residential street. There were three cars and a bus involved in a pile-up at the junction, one car having been forced from the road and through the front wall of a house. The blackened scars of an old fire blistered one flank of the bus, but it was impossible to tell whether this was a result of the accident, or something that had happened afterwards.

Jack caught his breath and glanced at Emily. *I never really considered*, he thought. *All the* bodies *we might see, all the* dead. But Sparky was already running for the bus, raising his hand and whistling in a grim parody of a late commuter.

Lucy-Anne chuckled.

The boy forced his way through the half-open door and looked around, only his silhouette visible against the dust-streaked windows. He jumped off again quickly. "No one home!" he shouted. "But someone's been shopping in Harrods."

"Anything worth having?" Jenna asked.

Sparky stood before them, blinking, the ruin of the vehicles behind him. "It's not my stuff to look at," he said.

"I know someone who went to Harrods soon after Doomsday," Rosemary said. "He came out with a diamond necklace and a hand-sized horse carved from soap. Three days later he threw the necklace away and started washing."

She was serious, but for some reason Lucy-Anne found what she said unbearably amusing. She started giggled, then laughing, bending over with hands on her knees and roaring at the pavement.

"Quiet!" Rosemary said, but if Lucy-Anne heard, she did not care. The laughter continued, and Jack could not find it in himself to try and stop her. She'd been acting differently ever since the dog attack, and it felt good to see her like this. He tried to shove the fact that she might be losing it to one side.

"Lucy-Anne!" Rosemary said, angry at first, but quickly growing calmer. The woman touched the girl's back, smoothing softly as the laughter changed quickly into tears. "We need to be quiet. Really, we do. London is a dangerous place now, dear. There's more than just people that will do us harm."

Lucy-Anne stood and moved away from Rosemary, wiping her eyes, looking around at the group then away again. *She's still messed up*, Jack realised. *That was no release for her at all. She needs . . . something.*

Rosemary looked at the sky to the west, where oranges and reds bled across rooftops. "We should go," she said. "I don't like crossing the Barrens in the dark."

"Why?" Jenna asked.

"They're haunted."

Jack had never believed in ghosts, but her words struck a chill in his heart. Emily clasped his hand and he squeezed back.

They followed Rosemary along the street, past the crashed cars and bus and towards the junction at the far end. It felt strange walking past so many silent houses, and Jack thought this was what Rosemary meant by being haunted. She'd said that the Barrens was a grave, but wasn't the whole of London now one big tomb? He thought of what the houses to his left and right contained, how many of the inhabitants had probably died at home and still sat or lay there now, staring at the sunset-streaked windows with skullish eyes. It was chilling, and the silence made it doubly so. Any place so used to noise and bluster became haunted when it was silent and still. He remembered when his father had remained behind at work one evening to finish a report, and the strange look in his eyes when he came home. When Jack had asked what was wrong, he'd simply said, *I'm used to the building being full.*

"These places feel full of the dead," Jack whispered, his voice carrying in the silence.

"Not all of them," Rosemary said. "There were efforts to clean up. The government right at the beginning, and then us. We couldn't just let the city rot."

"Then where . . . ?" As Jack spoke they rounded the corner at the end of the street, and his question was answered.

Lucy-Anne had never seen a place that looked so wrong. It reminded her of the Exclusion Zone, but the space before them had not only been flattened, but apparently excavated and turned as well, as if to expose fresh ground to the new world. No old buildings remained standing, though there *were* structures out there, ambiguous and strange in the fading light. It was maybe a mile across in both directions. Shrubs and sapling trees grew in abundance, lush and somehow grotesque. She could not work that out. Leaves shone with health, flowers were full and fat, yet she could not shake the idea that they were *wrong*.

"It's a mass grave," Jack said.

"Yes," Rosemary replied. "The Barrens. The area was destroyed in a huge blaze two days after Doomsday. It didn't take much for them to finish the job."

"A grave?" Emily said. She was still filming. "How can that be a grave?"

"No one knows how many are buried here," Rosemary said. "Twenty thousand? A hundred thousand? A million?"

"Those plants . . ." Lucy-Anne began, wondering whether talking about them would reveal why they looked so disturbing. *I've seen them before*, she thought, and a memory promised itself to her . . . but not yet.

"They look almost meaty," Sparky said, and yes, that was it, and when Lucy-Anne closed her eyes and breathed in deeply she could almost smell the rawness of them.

"Fertile ground," Jack said. Lucy-Anne knew what he meant, and it was dreadful.

"We have to cross that?" Jenna asked.

Rosemary nodded. "I've done it many times before. But never in the dark."

"Because it's haunted?" Emily's voice was small and lost.

"There's no such things as ghosts," Jack said, squeezing his sister's shoulder.

"You don't need ghosts for a place to feel haunted," Rosemary said. "Please, come on. The light's fading."

They went, and as they passed from the neat, paved areas of a dead London street and onto the heaved ground of the Barrens, Lucy-Anne wondered if everyone was thinking thoughts similar to hers: *My family could be beneath my feet right now.*

When she closed her eyes, she saw their death-masks grinning up at her from mass graves. She ground her teeth together to shove away the image. A nightmare? She thought not. Just her imagination going overdrive, and she determined to walk on.

The ground was uneven. Smooth here, ridged and cracked there, sunken elsewhere, it promised broken bones for the unwary. Lucy-Anne looked all around, searching for the glint of bones, or the messy trail of hair still attached to shrunken scalps. But whoever had done the burying had been thorough.

"We're walking on them," Jenna said, something like fascination in her voice. Nobody replied.

They passed the first spread of lush plants, and Lucy-Anne could not identify them. The shrubs' flowers looked like roses, but from the stems below the flowers hung catkins, and the thorns were long and thin like hawthorn. Lower down, a bright red heather hugged the ground, spread through the cracks and crevasses like something spilled. She thought of asking whether anyone recognised the species, but decided against it. She was afraid that they were new. Now that Sparky had used the term *meaty*, Lucy-Anne could not shake that impression from her mind when she breathed in. And the flowers themselves were heavy, damp, brightly coloured. *Fertile ground*, Jack had said, and Lucy-Anne tried in vain to not visualise what lay beneath.

"A marker," Rosemary said as they approached a low structure. "There are lots of them. Sometimes you'll even find fresh flowers here." The structure was surprisingly well-made, constructed from red London bricks and painted around its circular base with a thick black coating. Its round top was slightly sloped to allow water to run off, but embedded in the surface was a glass-enclosed picture, still sharp and clear even though moisture had penetrated through a crack in one corner. The man stared up at them as they passed, smiling happy thoughts from a vanished time.

"How do they know exactly where he was buried?" Jenna asked. "It must have been . . ."

"They used army wagons mostly," Rosemary said. "Sometimes removal lorries. Brought them here by the hundreds. I never saw it myself, but I've heard accounts, and it doesn't take much to imagine. So you're right, dear. No one can know for sure where any particular body is buried. I think those that come here treat it like one grave."

*One grave*, Lucy-Anne thought, and a flash of memory stabbed at her again. Again, she drove it away.

"Dead London," Sparky said. "Bloody freaking me out, I know that for sure."

"There are some rough paths to follow. We'll be across in a few minutes." Rosemary looked nervously back the way they had come, where the sun was just disappearing below a line of rooftops.

Her nervousness unsettled Lucy-Anne even more. *She can't really mean it's haunted?* She looked around at the grotesque, strange surroundings, and the silence that enclosed them felt like a held breath. What sounds the Barrens would utter once darkness fell, she had no wish to discover.

They passed more memorials of all shapes, sizes, and designs. One was constructed in cast concrete, eight feet tall and six wide, and three names were carved lovingly into its surface. Another was a brick-built square thirty feet across, the ground within flattened and planted as a perfect lawn, a small wooden cross at its centre. Whoever had built it obviously maintained it, as the grass was trimmed and the cuttings strewn beyond the wall. There were countless wooden markers; many crosses, and others simply stakes driven into the ground. Pictures were pinned to some of them, the majority faded and leached of colour by the sun, but some obviously replaced frequently. Others had names carved into them. As well as the brick or stone markers, there were other elaborate sculptures of twisted and shaped metal that would not have looked out of place in an art gallery.

*They could be here*, Lucy-Anne thought. Every step she took was painful, and the silence from the rest of the group testified to their upset as well. Among them all, Jack and Emily were the lucky ones. They had family, and everyone else walked alone.

"Oh," Rosemary said. She paused, glanced back and then continued walking. Perhaps the sun was sinking too quickly for her to think about changing their course.

Someone or something had excavated a hole thirty feet from the rough path they were following. Soil and broken masonry had been dug through to reach the softer parts beneath, and in the dusky light the spread of bones looked pink. There were skulls in there, and leathery skin, and hair twisted across stretched features.

Lucy-Anne fell to her knees. Something about this place was so familiar, and yet her memory teased her still. *Just do it!* she thought, challenging her nightmares to strike her once again. But if they *did* have something to say about this place, they held back.

For the next couple of minutes they had to step over and around a mess of bones splayed across the path. Some of them bore teeth marks. Others had been chewed through to get to the good stuff inside.

Rosemary led them on, and as daylight fled and gave the Toxic City back to the night, they left that sad, surreal place and found themselves once more in familiar streets.

They gathered in a small square where once-tended plants had grown wild, and where birds chattered as they chose their roosts for the night.

"It's not far now," Rosemary said. "There's a house two streets away that I sometimes use. There's food there, and bottled water, and enough rooms—"

"Listen!" Sparky held up his hand, eyes wide, head tilted to one side. The birds had also fallen silent, equally attuned to the sound of danger. "Engines."

"Quickly!" Rosemary led them across the road and through a gate into the small park at the square's centre. "Hide, stay low, and whatever you do, make sure you're not seen."

"Choppers?" Jenna asked.

"Almost certainly. Irregulars hardly ever use vehicles."

Lucy-Anne hid with Jack and Emily behind a bank of undergrowth growing around an old oak tree. She looked for the others but they had all hidden themselves away so well that even she could no longer see them. She had the crazy idea that they had never been there at all.

"I'm afraid," Emily said.

The motors were drawing closer. There were several of them, and above their grumble he heard the distinctive sound of something else: a helicopter.

"Me too." Lucy-Anne smiled at the girl.

"But we're here," Jack whispered into his sister's ear. "We're in London, and Mum and Dad will be here too."

"Yeah," she said, smiling. "Do you think they'll remember us?"

Jack tried to answer, but his voice broke. "Shh," he said instead. He glanced at Lucy-Anne and she saw tears in his eyes. "Shh."

The helicopter passed overhead. She saw it through the jagged branches of the oak tree, its tail light flashing red as it hovered briefly, then thundered away across the Barrens. It was too high for its downwash to be felt, but so loud that Lucy-Anne could not even hear her own breathing. She noticed that though Emily cringed into her brother, her right hand was held out from her side, the dark lens of the camera facing up.

As the helicopter drifted away, the square was illuminated by a flood of headlamps. Lucy-Anne tried to hunker down lower, gasping as the light fingered through bushes and between tree trunks to briefly dazzle her. The engine sound did not change. She heard heavy wheels grinding on the gritty road, and another set of headlamps swung through to follow the first. The two vehicles grumbled around the square, their engine noise intensely threatening. But behind them, a heavier sound. It rumbled and shook through the ground as well as through the air, and it made leaves in the square shake where the helicopter could not.

"What's that?" Emily asked.

"Don't know. Big truck." Lucy-Anne peered through the bushes, trying to make out the shape and size of the two vehicles driving around the edge of the square. They seemed quite small, but before she could get a good look, they were gone, and the massive rumble that followed them took over.

It echoed from the buildings around the square, shook the ground, and the lights—red, yellow, and white—slashed through the undergrowth as if it was not there. It ended the shadows in that place, and its motor sounded angry and hungry.

The vehicle turned around the edge of the square, following the two smaller trucks that had preceded it. Through branches and past heavy limbs draped with leaves, Lucy-Anne could see its shape, and it was huge. It reminded her of an oil tanker, but its heavy grey sides looked daunting, the three conical towers on its back ugly and threatening with the stubby black guns that protruded from them.

The engine tone lowered for a moment and she thought it was going to slow.

"They *can't* have seen us!" Emily said, almost shouting to be heard.

Lucy-Anne delved into her pocket for the knife Sparky had let her keep, laughing out loud at how ineffective it felt.

Then the giant vehicle lumbered on, putting on a surprising spurt of speed as it skirted the square and disappeared after the 4x4s.

For a couple of minutes after the lights disappeared and the vehicles were out of sight, everyone remained where they were. Lucy-Anne listened to the engines fading away, echoes coming back at them and playing tricks with direction and distance. Then Rosemary crawled across to them, her eyes wide, fearful, and perhaps excited as well. "Choppers!" she said. "And that big monster was one of their mobile labs. I've watched Irregulars taken into there, never to be seen again."

"We need to go to your house," Jack said. Emily was still shivering in his arms. "It's been a long day, Rosemary, and we need rest. This is all too much."

"Near miss, eh?" Sparky said, crawling across to them.

"Got it all on here, I think," Emily said, holding up her camera and smiling weakly.

"There won't be another patrol for a while," Rosemary said.

"I need to find my family," Lucy-Anne whispered. Her heart was thrumming, and something had started ticking deep inside her, a timer slowly running out of sand. She was counting down to something, and she had no idea what.

"Not yet," Jack said.

"Lucy-Anne, we need—" Jenna began.

"My *family*!" she said, louder this time. "We've come all this way, been through those bloody tunnels . . . those *dogs*! And I'm not just going to go to fucking sleep!"

"Quiet!" Rosemary said.

"Stop telling me to be quiet, old woman!"

"Lucy-Anne." Jack stepped forward and held her arms, trying to pull her close. She resisted, pulling back, staring over Jack's shoulder at something more distant.

"Where did they live?" Rosemary said. Her voice was calmer now, cooler.

Lucy-Anne glanced at her, but said nothing.

"Answer her," Jack said. "She knows the city."

"She led us to those dogs."

"Tooting, wasn't it?" Jenna asked. "Didn't they live near the big police station in Tooting?"

Rosemary sighed and lowered her head.

"What?" Lucy-Anne demanded. "What the hell does that mean?"

"Tooting isn't there anymore," Rosemary said softly. "We just walked across it, and now it's called the Barrens."

Lucy-Anne gasped, and her defences fell from her in a heartbeat. She crumpled in Jack's arms, slumping down as though her knees had given out. She wished he could hold her tight enough to stop everything, just for a while.

"It doesn't mean they're dead," he whispered in her ear.

*No, they're not dead*, she thought. And something deep inside seemed to grin.

She pulled away from Jack and stood on her own. She smoothed down her clothes, ran her fingers through her hair, and wiped an errant tear from her cheek. Then she glanced at Rosemary. "Sorry." The word was quiet, but they all heard it in the silence.

Rosemary nodded and gave a brief smile. "We should go. If we hurry, we can be there before it's fully dark."

They followed the woman out of the square and along a narrow street, as they had been following her all that long day. She had led them out of the world they knew and into one they used to know, but which was now a mysterious, dangerous place. She had healed their wounds after the dogs attacked them, and told them about the strange places beneath London, both old and new. She had walked them across the largest grave the world had ever seen, and pointed out monuments to individual people that seemed, in Lucy-Anne's eyes at least, to be more immediate than the thought of a million dead.

She trusted the old woman, and she didn't. She liked her, and she feared her. And as Rosemary unlocked the front door to an innocuous, terraced house in a street that had once sung with life, Lucy-Anne wondered whether history was too powerful for any of them to change.

# CHAPTER NINE
# SPECK

There will be a statement from the prime minister on all TV and radio channels at 10:00 p.m.

—*Government Statement, all-channel broadcast, 8:15 p.m. GMT, July 28, 2019*

It was a normal house, its owners dead or gone since Doomsday. Rosemary had tacked several layers of thick sheets and blankets over every window and door so that she could light candles without being seen. There were a few lighter patches on the papered walls where pictures had once hung, empty book cases, and piled in a small room at the rear of the house were a pram, bouncy chair, and several bags of baby toys and clothes. She told them that she had tried to depersonalise the house—not to make it her own, but to make it anonymous.

Before Doomsday, she had been a nurse. She did not like stealing someone else's home.

Jack thought they would all have trouble falling asleep. After eating food cold from tins, Rosemary showed them to separate rooms. Lucy-Anne, Jenna, and Sparky took one, while Jack and Emily had another, bickering briefly about who should have the top bunk.

"It's dangerous," Jack said, and Emily laughed and climbed the ladder.

But when the time for sleep came, Jack closed his eyes and suffered none of the anxieties he feared. He had worried that being here at last, in the Toxic City, would keep them all awake. But he soon heard Sparky mumbling in his sleep and Emily's gentle breathing above him, and before dropping off himself he realised that the dangers of this place extended far beyond the ruins of the Exclusion Zone. London was perilous, but a world where such lies could be told, and such wonders hidden away, was deadly through and through.

For the past two years, none of them had ever been safe.

Breakfast was more cold food from tin cans, but baked beans had never tasted so good. Jack wondered how the Irregulars stayed healthy without anything fresh: no vegetables, fruit, or meat. But he kept having to remind himself that they were not normal people. *She's moved on*, he thought, watching Rosemary opening several large plastic bottles of water. *She's evolved, all of a sudden*. Her hands moved smoothly, confidently, the patterns they made almost poetic. What must it be like to have such power? He could barely imagine.

"I'm taking you to a man called Gordon," she said. "He's a friend, but not as . . . accepting of his new gift as I am."

"What's his gift?" Jack asked.

"He can trace bloodlines," she said. "One drip of blood, and he can sense it all across the city."

"You mean he can smell our families?" Sparky asked.

"It's much more than smell, dear," Rosemary said, smiling. She held up her hands. "Just as this is a lot more than touch."

"You're superheroes. Like Batman." Emily chewed on stale breadsticks, and her seriousness made them laugh. All except Rosemary. Jack noticed that she looked pained rather than amused, and he wondered just how accepting she really was.

"Yeah!" Jenna said. "Shouldn't you call yourself 'Healer,' or something? And your friend Gordon, he should be 'Sniffer'!"

"I prefer the name my parents gave me," Rosemary said.

"Still . . ." Jenna said, glancing around and catching Jack's eye. He saw the twinkle of amusement there, looked away quickly, and Lucy-Anne was staring right at him. He smiled but her expression did not change. Even when he leaned sideways in his chair, her eyes did not waver. Yet again, she was seeing something very far away.

"So where does Sniffer live?" Sparky asked.

"Gordon is one of the few I know who stays in the same place. It's a hotel, the London Court, and he has the top floor."

"All of it?"

"All of it. Why not? Apparently, Paul McCartney stayed there a few years ago, hired the whole top floor of the hotel for his entourage. Gordon quite likes that idea, so he's done it as well. Except he hasn't had to pay."

"And he feels safe staying in the same place?" Jack asked. "Safe from the Choppers?"

"Of course," Rosemary smiled. "He can smell trouble a mile away."

"Hah!" Sparky laughed. "Sniffer!"

"Please don't call him that to his face," Rosemary said, suddenly serious. "He knows what he can do, but . . . he doesn't like doing it."

"Why not?" Emily asked. "That seems daft. If you can do something special, you should."

"Well, dear, he finds it quite frightening."

Emily looked at Jack and blinked, and he could almost hear the cogs turning in her mind. *How awful to have something that scares you so much.*

"But he'll help?" he asked.

"Oh, I'm sure. He wants things to change as much as any of us."

They gathered some food and drink together and shared it around their rucksacks, then waited in the hallway behind the front door while Rosemary checked that the coast was clear. She'd told them that they would be staying to the side streets, alleys, and residential roads, as Chopper patrols concentrated more on the old shopping districts.

"It's quiet," she said, clicking the door shut again. "I'll go first, you follow in a close line."

"How far?" Jenna asked.

"A mile," Rosemary said. "Maybe less."

"What will we be seeing out there?" Lucy-Anne's voice was low and tense, as if she was waiting for something to happen. Jack had tried several times that morning to approach her, talk to her, but she had shrugged him off. He wondered whether they were even together anymore, and guessed not. Perhaps they never really had been.

His concern seemed so childish. And that made his sadness feel all the more indulgent.

"I know the route," the Irregular said. "Hopefully, nothing."

*Hopefully*. Jack squeezed his sister's hand and she beamed at him, full of the fresh new day. Kids. He wished he hadn't had to grow up so damn fast.

They walked the streets of London, past silent homes containing dark secrets, across roads that were already cracked with the soft green force of shoots tired of biding their time, passing shadows hunkered down in alleys and gardens like memories waiting to strike back at those who had made them bad, and for the first time Jack really understood the tragedy of what had happened. It struck him hard, and looking around at his friends he could believe that they were experiencing the same thoughts. Before today, back in Camp Truth, there had been mourning for their missing families and anger at the cover-up perpetuated by the government and military. That's where all their thoughts and emotions had gone, all their mental energy spent mourning and hating, grieving and conspiring—personal things, all tied to them.

None of them had ever really spared a thought for London.

This once-great city was now a ruin. True, buildings still stood straight and square, but the life was gone from here. Each darkened window in a house's façade promised only sadness contained within. The streets showed their age, now, without people and vehicles to pin them to the present. London was London no more, but a fading echo of what it had once been. A dead city.

Feeling sad, sensing London's history growing wilder, older, and further beyond redemption with every missed heartbeat, Jack walked with the others and let the sights and sounds wash over him.

They saw a family of foxes sitting and playing beside a road. The adults looked their way, but they remained on the street, when two years before they would have scampered away to wherever the city foxes hid during daylight. The cubs yapped and rolled, snapping at waving fern fronds growing along the gutter. Emily turned her camera their way, and as if aware of what she was doing, the wild animals fled, and the street felt as though they had never been there at all.

"Lots more foxes," Rosemary said. "And rabbits, badgers, weasels, squirrels, and rats."

"Food for the dogs, at least," Lucy-Anne said.

"It's becoming a wilder place to live." The woman smiled at Emily's camera and then nodded along a narrow alley between two houses. "That way. There's a body down here, but you won't see much of it."

The skeleton was almost completely subsumed by nettles and ferns, the stalks and leaves sprouting up between ribs and through eye sockets. Jack wanted to walk straight by, but Emily paused and moved some of the plants aside with her foot. She started a quiet commentary into her camera's microphone.

"Who was this sad person, dead in an alley, killed by the lies told to everyone? They had long hair that might have been blonde, like mine. A leather jacket. A badge on the jacket, saying how much they liked the Dropkick Murphys, and a T-shirt, but it's too faded to see what was written on it. Did they fall here and die quickly, or crawl from a long way away? Were they coming from somewhere, or trying to get somewhere else?" She trained the camera along the body, then stepped away and let the ferns spring back up. "Another grim statistic of the Toxic City."

"Come on, Emily," Jack said. She looked at him, scared.

"This could have been us, if we'd come with Mum and Dad. This could have been *anyone*. We might have been friends."

"Come on."

Within twenty minutes of leaving the house, Jack craved the sight of another human being. Rosemary led them along side-streets, through alleys, and, at one point, over several garden walls and through the small enclosed places that had once been so private and contained. He felt like an intruder, passing across family spaces once used as play areas for children, or barbeque areas for their parents. He saw children's garden toys hidden amongst the long grass and shrubs gone wild, and in one garden he noticed that the French doors leading into the house were open a few inches. He tried to see inside, but a slick green moss covered the inner surface of the glass, turning everything into shadow. He did not feel watched.

"Where are the other Irregulars?" he asked Rosemary as they paused beside an overturned lorry. It had been carrying boxes and boxes of books, the last bestseller now swollen into unreadable humps all across the road.

"We've been seen," Rosemary said. "There was one in a house just back there, watching from an upstairs window."

"Did you know them?"

"Don't think so. They'd have probably said hello if I did."

"So is everyone alone, now?" he asked. "Is this how it always is?"

"Oh, no, Jack," she said, apparently surprised at how he felt. "I do have *some* friends. There are people I see regularly, people I mix with. Many of us live on our own most of the time, of course, because it's far safer that way. But we have . . . not really a community, but an existence. There's plenty of hide and seek, but the Choppers don't bother us constantly. We just have to keep watch for them. And there are Irregulars with gifts that can do that for us."

"So when do we meet Gordon?" he asked, feeling his friends' eyes upon him as well as the lens of Emily's camera. "It's not just Lucy-Anne who wants to know about her family."

"It's not far now. We have to cross a couple of main streets, but we'll be fine."

"No dogs?" Lucy-Anne asked. "Wolves, lions, bears?"

"I've never heard of a bear being seen south of the river," Rosemary said, and Jack was not sure whether she was joking.

They crossed the main roads carefully, running in pairs, and very little changed. Jack saw a dozen cats sitting together in front of one smashed-up shop, licking their paws, lazing in the sun and watching the humans rush across the street. It was an unsettling sight, because he'd never seen more than two cats sitting together before. It was as if the loss of their erstwhile owners had given them free reign to exist and adapt as they wished.

After the main roads, Rosemary led them along a lane beside a tall, grand looking building. Several cars had been burnt out here, and they had to climb over the scorched metallic ruins because there was no room between the walls. Jenna slipped on the last car and gasped as raw metal sliced her ankle.

"I'll see to that in a minute," Rosemary said, and Jack stared at her with amazement once again.

Past the cars, the woman opened a heavy grille gate, which had a chain and padlock placed around it as though locked. When the others filed through after her she replaced the chain, hanging the padlock so that it did not quite click shut.

Jenna groaned, leaning on Sparky for support. Blood dripped from her boot.

"At least he'll have smelled us by now," Rosemary said, kneeling beside the wounded girl.

"Make him sound like a bloody vampire," Lucy-Anne said.

"There's no such things as vampires," Rosemary muttered, and that made them all laugh softly. She looked up, surprised at first, and then smiling along with them. "Fair enough," she said. "Maybe there are, and I just haven't met them yet. London's full of secrets."

She rested Jenna's foot against her leg and touched the cut, growing still and silent as her fingers did their work.

A door opened behind them. Something long and dark emerged, aiming their way, and behind it was the most terrified face Jack had ever seen.

"It's me!" Rosemary said, jumping up and holding up both hands, the right one still bloody. "Gordon, it's me."

The man behind the gun blinked and looked at all of them, one by one. "They're from outside!" he said.

"Yes, of course. I told you I was going."

"But I never thought you'd come back." Gordon lowered the gun slightly, and a smile struggled to break his expression. But he still looked frightened. "Come inside, quickly. There's been lots of patrols. I'm sure they know I'm here."

"If they knew, they'd have come for you by now," Rosemary said. "It's nice to see you, Gordon."

He swing the rifle down by his side, and at last the smile looked almost at home. "And you."

Rosemary went first, and the others followed, with Gordon closing the door behind Jenna and throwing bolts, turning a key and clipping shut two heavy padlocks.

"Nothing like home security," Sparky said.

"Peace of mind," the man said. "That's all it gives me." He was a short, thin man, with closely shaven hair, a small goatee and piercing blue eyes. He looked exhausted, with dark bags under his eyes and heavy jowls. But Jack guessed he always looked like that, and probably had before Doomsday. He wondered what Gordon had been: Stock trader? Doctor? Shop keeper? He almost asked, but decided he didn't really need to know something so buried in the past. Nobody was what they used to be.

Gordon's eyes also looked haunted, as if he already knew why they had come to see him.

They followed him through the kitchens, store rooms, and back-of-house areas of the hotel, eventually coming to the service staircase that took them up twelve flights and six floors. By the end of the climb Sparky and Jenna were panting, and Lucy-Anne grinned at them both.

"You need more exercise!" she said. Emily was filming her, and she gave the camera two thumbs-up. Jack was pleased to see her smile.

"Give me a second," Gordon muttered, disappearing through a door and leaving them alone on the top landing.

"Where's he gone?" Jenna asked.

"Security measures," Rosemary said. "He must like you all." They heard some strange noises from beyond the door—a whirring sound, clicking, and the clinking of dozens of bottles—and then the door opened and Gordon peered around the jamb.

He offered them a weak smile. "Welcome to my humble abode."

The door opened onto the junction of two long corridors, perpendicular to each other. From the décor, carpet, furniture, and mirrors placed along the corridor, Jack could tell immediately that this had once been a plush hotel.

They followed Gordon along the left hand corridor, passing a complex arrangement of bottles, wires, and metallic stands that he must have just decommissioned. Jack wondered whether it was just a warning system, or something more sinister.

Gordon unlocked the door and waved them into a room.

"What's this, the Presidential Suite?" Sparky asked, but beneath the bluff and bluster, Jack could sense his awe.

The room was huge. It contained the largest bed Jack had ever seen, and even that was swallowed by the space, standing on a pedestal to one side and surrounded by a heavy oak four-poster frame and fine drapery. There was a large seating area with three full-sized sofas, a dining table that would probably sit a dozen people, and close to the main panoramic window there was a sunken area scattered with low tables, floor cushions, and what looked like a small water fountain.

"So, where's everyone else sleeping?" Sparky asked, leaping onto the bed. He wriggled his eyebrows at Jenna and patted the covers beside him, and she gave him the finger.

Emily giggled and aimed her camera somewhere else.

"I've never slept in here," Gordon says. "There are several side rooms, and I have one of those. More than enough for me. But I do spend a lot of my time sitting here, reading, looking out over London . . ." He wandered across to the far wall, stepping down in to the sunken area and standing before the huge window.

"Can't you be seen from outside?" Jenna asked.

"Reflective glass. The only way anyone out there will see in is if I light this place up at night, and I never do that. A candle in the bedroom, that's all I allow."

"Plumbing still work?" Lucy-Anne asked.

"Not for over a year."

"Oh."

Gordon turned around and smiled apologetically, and Jack thought he was enjoying this human contact. Maybe talking to people without having to wonder at their advanced, evolved powers was a refreshing change. "There's somewhere you can go down the corridor, room 608. The bath's filled with water and a bucket. Not the most luxurious of flushes, but it works well enough."

Lucy-Anne nodded her silent thanks but remained where she stood. There was an awkward silence. Gordon glanced around at them all, and Jack saw something pass across his face, the shadow of the same haunted expression he'd seen downstairs. *He knows what's coming, and he hates it*.

"Gordon," Rosemary said, "you did something for me a long time ago, and now these people need your help in the same way."

Gordon nodded, then sat down slowly on a pile of floor cushions. "They know how it works?"

"Not exactly," she said.

*I wonder what he saw of Rosemary's family*, Jack thought, but right then it did not seem like something he could ask. Maybe later.

"I'll go first," Sparky said. He hopped from the bed, crossed the room, and dropped down beside Gordon. "Name's Sparky," he said, holding out his hand.

"Pleased to meet you, Sparky." Gordon shook.

"Yeah, well, you don't look that pleased, mate. But my brother, he was here when it happened. And Rosemary said you can help. And I'd really . . . I want to . . ." Sparky trailed off. Jack had never seen his friend looking so scared. He could face wild dogs and drunken men looking for a brawl, but now he was close to the truth about his brother Stephen, and reality these days was known to bite.

"I can try," Gordon said. "None of us can work miracles, and I never promise anything. But I can try." He looked at Rosemary strangely then, frowning and glancing around at Jack and his friends.

"They know," Rosemary said. "They've already had cause to see what I can do."

Gordon slumped down, almost as though the cushions were swallowing him up. "Well then, Sparky, I'll need a drip of your blood."

Sparky pulled his knife and flicked it open.

"Just a speck," Gordon said.

Jack and Emily went forward, as did Jenna and Lucy-Anne. The air of the large room suddenly became heavy and uncomfortable, as though there were too many people breathing at the same time, and that reminded Jack of his strange dream of following his mother along the airless street.

"Are we really ready for this?" Jack said, and foolish as the question sounded to him, nobody treated it as such.

"I think so," Sparky said.

Emily nodded.

"I am," Lucy-Anne said.

"Good luck," Jenna said. "Really, all of you. I should leave."

"No!" Jack said. "You didn't lose anyone on Doomsday, but you're part of our gang."

"Right!" Lucy-Anne said.

"Yeah." Sparky nodded, then prodded the knife at his left thumb. He hissed, then stared at the dribble of blood that bloomed and then flowed down his hand and onto his wrist.

Gordon leaned forward, hand held out. "May I?"

Sparky offered this stranger, this Irregular, his shaking hand.

Gordon touched the wound on Sparky's thumb with his index

finger, just enough to pick up a smear of blood. Then he went to the huge window and pulled on a cord, opening five fanlights at ceiling level. A breath of fresh air and the cooing of pigeons came in, and Gordon put the bloodied finger into his mouth.

They all watched him, and he must have sensed it because he lowered his head as he withdrew his finger. Jack edged to one side, trying to see the man's expression, and then he wished he'd remained where he was.

Gordon was cringing, almost gagging, as though he'd put something rotten and rank onto his tongue, rather than a droplet of a living person's blood. A tear squeezed from his eyes and spotted the expensive carpet at his feet.

Jack saw Rosemary's face drop, and she looked down at her feet. *He knows*, he thought. *She's seen this reaction before.*

"His name's Stephen," Sparky said. "He lived in Peckham, last I heard. Taller than me." Gordon did not react to his voice, and Jack could see desperation creeping over his friend. "Tattoo on his arm. His name." He stood and approached the man, reaching out but pausing just before he touched the Irregular's shoulder.

"I'm sorry," Gordon said, "but your brother's dead."

Jack expected shouting and raving, denial and fury, and for a second he saw that and more behind Sparky's eyes. All that, and the temporary madness of grief.

But then Sparky stepped away from Gordon and slumped back down onto the floor cushions, holding his head in his hands and trying to cover his eyes, his ears, trying to shut himself off from the cruel world that had destroyed his family and left him like this.

Jack wanted to go to him. He saw Jenna take a step forward as well. But Emily grasped his hand, and Jenna looked at Lucy-Anne, then across at him. Being the one out of all of them who had not had family in London, she was aware that there could be more grief to come.

"Me next," Lucy-Anne said. Her voice was gruff. She jumped down beside Sparky, snatched the knife from his hand and drew the blade harshly across her palm. She hissed and grimaced, and blood spattered the cushions and carpet as she strode to Gordon.

"I only need a speck," Gordon said.

"Take as much as you want."

She held out her hand.

*There are wolves howling in the distance . . .*

Her hand was shaking, she couldn't help that. Part of it was the pain of the cut, but most of it was because of what this man could do. What he was *going* to do. He moved closer and dabbed a finger in her blood, and Lucy-Anne squeezed her eyes shut.

*Closer by, between clumps of exotic plants, a more level spread of ground . . .*

"I've dreamed this," she whispered, and if any of the others heard her, they said nothing.

She watched Gordon turn and approach the window again. He stepped so close that she saw his breath condensing on the glass. Then he took a deep breath and touched Lucy-Anne's blood to his tongue.

*. . . and deep down, the faces of the dead she still loves.*

"No," Lucy-Anne moaned, and she knew that nightmare at last.

Gordon cringed again, quivering in the sunlight slanting through the window. Then he grew still, and he spoke without turning around or looking up. "Your brother is alive north of here. The rest, I think you already know."

"No," she moaned again, hand clenching tight around the knife handle, her other hand dripping blood onto the lush carpet. "We walked over them. I could have seen them, I knew they were there . . ." The whole nightmare came to her now, a solid, dreadful memory that refused to go away.

She screamed, raised the knife again, saw the startled expressions on her friends' faces, and threw the blade over Sparky's head towards the bed. Even before it bounced from one of the corner posts she was running, screaming again, raging, venting fury and hatred as spittle-strewn invectives.

"We can't have her making too much—" she heard Gordon say.

"Her mum and dad are dead!" Emily snapped.

Lucy-Anne reached the door and hauled it open, swinging it so hard that the handle knocked a chunk from the plasterboard wall behind. She went with no destination in mind, bursting through doors, sprinting along corridors, trying to outrun the nightmare that had been stalking her since yesterday. And for a while, in that place of endless corridors and rooms that all looked the same, she lost herself to grief and rage.

As his girlfriend disappeared out into the corridor, and Sparky looked up as though he had never seen any of them before, Jack only wanted to hear about his father.

"You really need to stop her," Gordon said. "There are Superiors about, I sensed them earlier."

"Superiors?" Jack asked, confused.

"Later!" Rosemary said, grabbing Jack's arm. "Go after her." Lucy-Anne's screams were fading as she ran.

"But my father . . ." he said.

"I can tell you about him soon enough. And dear Susan, your mother. But stop her making that noise, or we'll all be in trouble."

*My father? My mother?*

Rosemary glared at Jack, and he nodded, signalling Emily to stay with the others and then running for the door.

Just as he exited the plush suite and started along the corridor, he heard Gordon say, "Oh sweet Jesus, they're already here."

# CHAPTER TEN
# REAPER

There will be a statement from the prime minister on all TV and radio channels at midnight.

—*Government Statement, all-channel broadcast,*
*10:30 p.m. GMT, July 28, 2019*

Jack expected monsters.

*"Superiors"? What the hell are they?*

As he ran along the plush hotel corridor in pursuit of Lucy-Anne's fading screams, he wondered whether he was now just following echoes.

*I've never heard of them, Rosemary never mentioned them, and—*

The door to the service staircase opened. Jack skidded to a halt.

A woman stepped out. She was beautiful, but terrifying in a way Jack could not properly establish. Maybe it was the complete disregard she seemed to have for her appearance: tatty, loose trousers; a torn jacket; dirty sweatshirt. Or perhaps it was her eyes and the way they seemed to bore right through him from the second they locked glances.

"Where are you going?" she asked, and her voice came from inside his head as well as without. Jack slumped against the wall.

"I'm following Lucy-Anne to bring her back," he said without thinking.

"Who's Lucy-Anne?"

"My girl . . ." He frowned, because that no longer seemed right. "My friend."

"Where are the others?"

*What others?* Jack thought. He could not lead this person—this Superior—to Emily, Sparky, and Jenna.

"Room 602," he said. Then he started backing away from this woman, because he had not intended to say anything.

"It's all right," she said, smiling. "You couldn't help yourself."

The door behind her opened again and a man stepped through, incredibly tall and exactly the opposite to her when it came to clothing. He wore an expensive suit, cuff links, a thin dark tie, and his shoes were shined to a mirror-like sheen. His face was very severe, and Jack's first thought was that the man would never be in danger of suffering laughter lines.

"Then I think you should go back to 602 to join them," the man said. He raised his right hand, as if to point back along the corridor.

"But I'm . . ." Jack began. The man's fingers flexed. Jack's right bicep twitched and clenched, and the muscles in his thigh contracted, like the worst case of cramp he'd ever had. He groaned and took a step back, feeling as though he'd been shoved.

The woman was smiling at him. Her eyes shone.

The man came forward, and Jack saw that he was limping, one leg of his trousers torn and dark with blood.

"I'm going," Jack said, and when the man lowered his hand the feeling of manipulation left.

Jack turned and ran. With every step, he listened out for more shouts and screams from Lucy-Anne. But she was either too far way for him to hear anymore, or she had at last seen or sensed the danger they were all in.

At the door to room 602 he paused and looked back. The woman was close, and behind her came the man, limping heavily but displaying no sign of pain in his expression. In fact, his grim face gave away nothing, and Jack had always been afraid of masks.

The door had not been closed properly, and just as the woman reached Jack it swung open, revealing Gordon and Rosemary standing just inside.

"We heard the noise," the woman said. "We'd like to join the party."

"You've no business here," Gordon said.

"No business?" the tall man replied, talking over Jack's head. "No business in this fine hotel, in this dead city, where law no longer reigns?" He leaned across Jack, his voice lowered. "The likes of you don't decide whose business is whose."

Jack could see panic in Rosemary's eyes, and he wondered just how dangerous these two Superiors were. He turned around. The woman was directly behind him, scruffy but beautiful, and she held him with her piercing gaze.

"We don't want trouble," Jack said, his voice bled weak by the effect she had upon him. She blinked, slow and sensuous.

The tall man looked down at him then, his face so close that Jack could smell his stale breath. "If you don't want trouble, boy, why find your way into London at all?"

"They're not from outside," Gordon said, "they come from—"

"Where are they from?" the woman asked.

"Outside," Gordon replied. He frowned and looked away.

"You're Superiors," Jack said. Perhaps if he could connect with them, things would not go so bad.

"And you're normal," the tall man said, with evident distaste.

"Yeah, sorry," Jack said. "I can't heal wounds or make people tell me the truth. No interest at all, me." He could see between Rosemary and Gordon now, and Emily, Jenna, and Sparky were gathered together in the sunken seating area inside the room. They all looked scared. He wondered what they had been told.

"I think we'll still come inside anyway, just to check things over," the Tall Man said. He pushed past Jack and into the hotel room.

Jack looked at the woman. She seemed to wear a permanent, cute smile. "After you," she said.

When they were all inside the room, the woman shut the door and locked it behind them.

"I'm Puppeteer," the tall man said.

"And I'm his beautiful assistant, Scryer." The woman by the door performed a small curtsey, lifting an imaginary skirt hem.

"Oh, very imaginative," Jack said.

Puppeteer glanced at him, then away again, as if dismissing Jack entirely from his consideration. He looked around the extravagant hotel suite, and then his attention rested on Jack's sister and friends. "Three more boring, unimportant people from outside, yes?"

"No, we come from—" Jenna began, but Jack stepped forward, taking the opportunity to join his friends. The air stank with danger.

"Don't bother," he said. He pointed at Scryer. "She can make you tell the truth."

"I can," the woman said, slinking across the room. Jack was amazed how sexy a woman could look in such innocuous clothing. "You told the truth about your ex-girlfriend, didn't you?"

Jack went cold. Such personal thoughts, exposed now for everyone. Scryer may have a lovely smile, but he could see the brutal potential in her ability.

"What do you two do?" Scryer asked.

Gordon and Rosemary answered at the same time. "I smell bloodlines . . ." "Healer . . ."

"Great powers!" Scryer said. "I've met lots of healers, of course, but it's still good. You're still special."

"But I'm not Superior," Rosemary said. Jack was surprised at the conviction in her voice.

"And why wouldn't you want to be?" Puppeteer asked. "You do something now you couldn't two years ago, doesn't that make you feel—"

"*I'm* still a human. Look at *you*! What was your real name? Paul? Derek? Now you call yourself Puppeteer, like some comic book hero?"

"I've moved on," Puppeteer said.

"Well, this is intense," Sparky whispered behind Jack. When Jack glanced around, Sparky and Jenna were standing close, Emily just in front of them.

"We'll be all right," Jack said.

"So what are outsiders doing in the Toxic City?" Scryer asked.

"Come to find my parents," Jack said, because it was true. He leaned forward, mouth working as if chewing on air, ready to tell these Superiors the rest of the reason they'd come here. But he swallowed the words and turned away. *So long as she gets* something *true,* he thought. Scryer was looking at him strangely, the smile now gone from her eyes. *And she knows that . . . she knows her limits!*

"Normals," Puppeteer sneered. "Just . . . humans."

"'Just'?" Jack asked. *So what's my mother?* he thought. *What's my father?* He looked at Rosemary but she would not meet his eyes.

"You're hurt," Rosemary said to the tall man.

"Someone shot me."

"Who?" Sparky asked. Puppeteer looked at him as though surprised he could even talk.

"A Chopper patrol, earlier today. We were playing with them, and they opened fire. Perhaps they forgot to have their coffee this morning."

"Is the bullet still inside?" Rosemary asked.

Puppeteer seemed uncertain about whether to even answer. Jack could see where this was heading; he could also sense the tall man's discomfort.

"Passed right through," Scryer answered for him.

"I can heal it," Rosemary said, but she made no move. *Waiting for permission*, Jack thought. *It's like Us and Them. Or Us, Them, and The Others.*

Puppeteer glanced down at his leg, trousers torn and shoe shining with fresh blood. He lifted his foot and turned it, wincing slightly as he put his weight on it once again. "Very well," he said. "I'll let you."

Rosemary knelt at Puppeteer's feet, and it was one of the strangest acts Jack had ever seen. The tall man turned away and stared through the tall, wide window. While Rosemary lifted the trouser leg and bunched it around his knee, exposing the wound so that she could work at it, the man sniffed, hummed to himself, and generally acted as though nothing was happening. His companion sat in one of the large sofas and called Gordon across to her, asking him questions in subdued tones. Jack could not hear what she said, but it was obvious by her continuing smile that the man was giving her the answers she sought. She kept glancing past the Irregular at Jack—none of the others, just him—and he felt the dreadful power of her gaze.

*I'd tell her the truth if she just looked at me*, he thought. He looked down at his shoes and thought about Lucy-Anne, crying and alone elsewhere in the hotel, or perhaps even out there, shouting her way through strange streets. He should be searching for her. But he knew they would not be allowed to leave.

"What will they do to us?" Emily whispered. She stepped closer to Jack, and he felt the cool angles of her camera against his leg.

"Nothing," he said. But he could not be certain of that at all. The Superiors pretended not to hear, but he was sure they had.

Rosemary knelt very still, apart from her fingers moving across and through the pouting wound. Jack could not see her face, but he had seen her doing this enough times before to know that it would be blank, cool, and in control. The man's hands hung by his sides, his fingers relaxed. Whatever powers he had were dormant, for now. But Jack could remember that alien sensation of his muscles twitching under someone else's command. Puppeteer, he called himself, and he thought himself Superior. Perhaps soon they would witness the full range of his abilities.

Jack glanced down again and realised that Emily was filming. The shock was cut through with respect for his sister. *Clever girl!* He looked up again, glancing from one Superior to the other, but he was certain she had not been seen.

He, his sister, and their friends had remained standing, frozen there by the Superiors' strange presence and the power they seemed to exude. But Jack realised that a lot of that effect was produced by their own sudden fears of what the Superiors would be, and what they would look like. It was a name Rosemary had never mentioned, something else she had kept from them, and they could not help letting fear run their imaginations into overdrive. Now, here were the Superiors: strong, aloof, but still very human. Whatever Doomsday had done to their minds and bodies, their humanity was still beyond doubt.

*Not monsters*, he thought. *No more than any other human being that does something inhuman.*

So he sat down, making his own choice to not be so entranced that he could not use his own mind. Scryer glanced past Gordon once again, her smile broadening as she looked at Jack, and he felt the stirrings of lust. God, but she was beautiful! Could she enter his mind? Is that how she dragged the truth from him, and others, with every question?

Sparky sat behind him, Jenna and Emily to his left. Emily had to rest the camera on her knees so that it peered above floor level. Jack knew that she would be noticed, eventually, if they had not clocked her already. And he feared for her. But he saw her excitement and delight, and he could share in what she was feeling. *Not so Superior*, he thought she was thinking. *Just people who think they're special enough to bully*.

"So you were hounding the Choppers?" Rosemary asked as she worked. Puppeteer looked down in surprise, as if he'd forgotten she was even there.

"Just for fun," he said.

"You hound them for fun, they come for us Irregulars. We're always easier to catch."

"Yes, but they only hurt you if we kill some of them."

"You really believe that?" she said. She stood and looked up into the tall man's face. "They take us and kill us as and when it pleases them. We're part of a research programme for them, right now. But when you and your Superior friends kill some of them, it becomes more than research. It becomes *revenge*!"

Puppeteer shrugged. He really did not care.

"Your leg's fixed," Rosemary said.

The tall man looked down at his leg, the gaping bullet wound now little more than a bruised patch on his skin. "Pity you can't fix suits. This one was expensive."

"You bought it?" Jenna asked. Jack drew in a sharp breath, but he also had to hold back a smile. This man's posturing, his arrogance, his disdain for those he saw as beneath him, all reminded him of a bully they'd once had in school. His name had been Kelly, and he'd delighted in throwing around his superior weight and pet-level intellect to hurt those smaller than him. Trouble was, *everyone* had been smaller than Kelly. At one time or another, virtually everyone in school had a run-in with him, boy or girl, first-year or sixth-year. He'd punched Jack once as he came down a staircase and Jack was walking up, giving him a swollen black eye and a dented pride. Jack, of course, had not struck back.

But every bully meets his match. Six boys caught Kelly after school one day, held him down, and beat him so hard they say he pissed blood. The violence shocked Jack, but Kelly seemed to shrink after that, though his rapid weight increase led to his nickname being changed to Bloater. Even Jack had called him that, and to his face as well. Small revenge, but sticks and stones . . .

Puppeteer looked at Jenna for some time, weighing up how, or even whether, to respond. "I'm a new man," he said at last. "I have no name other than Puppeteer. You can all hold onto the past, if you must. Old names, old values. So no, I did not buy this suit, little girl. I took it from a fine tailor's just off Oxford Street, and the owner was not there to object. If he or she had been, I would have moved them out of the way."

"Asshole," Sparky muttered.

Puppeteer lifted his hands then, fingers hanging like the readied legs of two large spiders. "Stop filming me," he said quietly, and his fingers flexed.

Emily was jerked up from her seat, the camera bouncing from a cushion and hitting the carpeted floor. Jack reached for her instinctively, but just as his hands closed around her ankles he felt a crippling pain in his upper arms, shards of agony thrust in from outside to slice through muscle and grate against bone. He fell back, and then Emily was above him, above all of them, held in mid-air and turning slowly, screaming, waving her arms and legs as she tried to swim back down.

"Jack!" she cried. "I can't . . . breathe! Can't . . ."

"Let her go!" Jack shouted, standing and spinning to face Puppeteer.

Rosemary had backed away, Scryer had stood from the big sofa—still smiling, still awfully beautiful—and the others were on their feet now as well, Sparky already trying to circle around past the bed so that he could get behind the tall Superior.

The little finger on Puppeteer's right hand twitched and Sparky cried out, his left leg cramping and folding beneath him. He grabbed his ankle and stared at the man, hate in his eyes.

Jack took one step forward and then Scryer was before him, a few steps away but close enough for him to see her excitement.

"Really want to get hurt?" she asked sweetly.

"Yes!" Jack spat. "For my sister, yes, and I don't need some shitty truth-witch to make me say that!" Scryer actually looked taken aback, and Jack felt a brief stab of delight.

Emily rose higher. Her head was almost touching the ceiling now, and her hands clawed at her throat. Her eyes were half-shut, and as she looked down at Jack a tear ran down her cheek.

"Please!" he said, trying to see past what Puppeteer had become to the humanity that must lie beneath.

But the man was enjoying this. He looked around the room, revelling in being the centre of things, not even needing to look at Emily to keep her suspended.

"Puppeteer, that's Reaper's daughter," Rosemary said quietly.

For the first time, doubt clouded Puppeteer's eyes. He tried to hide it—turned away, looked at Emily, glanced across at the wide view of the Toxic City—but Jack saw something touch Puppeteer then, and it looked very much like fear.

"Reaper," the man said.

Scryer's smile slipped for the first time.

"Who's Reaper?" Jack asked, confused.

Puppeteer dropped his hands and turned away, and Emily crashed to the floor. She gasped, a terrible, hoarse sound as she sucked in breath across her dry throat, and then she started crying.

"Bastard!" Jack shouted. Right then, if he'd had a gun he'd have fired it, if he'd had a knife he'd have thrown it. But he had neither, so he went to his sister and gathered her in his arms, nurturing the hate and letting it settle somewhere deep inside.

"Reaper," the man said again. He looked at them, shaking his head slowly. "Does he know?"

"Of course not," Rosemary said.

"We have to take them to him," Scryer said. "A gift. An honour!"

The tall man nodded.

"Who the bloody hell is Reaper?" Jack asked again.

Rosemary turned to him, glanced at Emily.

"Shit," Gordon said. "Shit, shit, now we're in even bigger trouble." He had moved across to the window, face raised as he sniffed at the air flowing through the fanlights.

"What is it?" Scryer asked.

"Choppers. Lots of them. And they've got a mobile lab wagon with them."

The scene in the posh hotel suite froze. The surreality of what was happening struck Jack, but he accepted it all. The Superiors, their strange powers, the old woman who could heal, Emily's harsh breathing, Sparky's anger still burning red in his cheeks. He accepted it because the world had changed so much. He'd known that since soon after Doomsday. Being here only crystallised that knowledge in his mind, and everything that happened now he would view through that altered perception.

"How do they know we're here?" Puppeteer asked.

"I don't know," Gordon said. He nodded at Scryer. "Why don't you get *her* to ask?"

Rosemary dashed to Emily's side, touching her throat and chest to see whether any healing was needed. The girl's eyes were open, her breathing becoming less harsh, and she groaned as she tried to talk.

"Okay . . . I'm okay . . ."

Jack hugged her tightly and kissed the top of her head. "Who's Reaper?" he asked Rosemary quietly, and she sighed.

"They're coming!" Scryer said. She was crouched at the window, and in the brief silence following her warning they could hear the sounds of engines.

Puppeteer looked at Jack and Emily, then stood up straight and smoothed down his suit. "They're everyone's enemy," he said, "so if you all listen to me, and do as I say, we may yet be able to escape."

"That's nice of you," Sparky said.

Puppeteer pointed at him, and Jack held his breath. *Smash him against the wall? Launch him from the window?* But as he held Sparky's full attention, the man spoke.

"If they catch you, they'll examine you to see why you have no trace of anything new. No powers, other than a big mouth. Got that, boy? They'll interrogate you first, then if they don't hear what they want to hear, they'll start cutting you up. Dissect your eyes and ears looking for any signs of mutation, your fingers and sexual organs, your heart. And then your brain. You do have a brain?"

Sparky glowered but said nothing.

"Good." Puppeteer nodded. "They'll come in the front way, slow and careful, because they don't know exactly who's in here. So we go back down the service staircase and out through the basement refuse doors."

"How do you know—?" Gordon began.

"We've been watching you for a while," Scryer replied.

"Come on," the tall Superior said. "Not much time." He waved them past him towards the door, and when Jack and Emily drew level he dropped in directly behind them. *Protecting us*, Jack thought, and try as he did he could not object to the idea.

*That's Reaper's daughter*, Rosemary had said. He tried to thrust that from his mind. He was frightened enough, for now.

Scryer went first, followed by Gordon and Rosemary. Sparky and Jenna brought up the rear. As they reached the staircase, they heard the first sounds of doors being kicked in several floors below.

"Slow and careful?" Jack whispered. Nobody replied.

Scryer opened the door to the service staircase, peeked inside and started descending. Two floors down, she paused and held up her hand, listening. She turned to Gordon.

He sniffed the air and nodded, pointing down the stairwell and holding up two fingers.

And then the door exiting the stairwell onto the fourth floor burst open, and the shooting began.

# CHAPTER ELEVEN
# MILLER

Stand by . . . stand by . . . stand by . . .

*—Message on every UK radio and TV channel,*
*midnight–6:00 a.m. GMT, July 29, 2019*

*Your brother is alive north of here . . .*

Lucy-Anne kept on running, enjoying the feeling of harsh breath in her chest, pain burning in her legs. She hit several doors that were locked and bounced from them, falling twice and rolling across the carpet, never growing still, never halting in her headlong flight, trying her utmost to leave behind the grief that had held her in its grasp for so long.

Outside London, she had held it at bay by being rebellious and non-conformist, holding onto hope by giving it wings. And here, now, in the Toxic City, something strange was happening, and her nightmares were becoming real.

Even so, she had fought against the truth.

But now that she knew—she had seen the rictus grins of her dead parents in her mind's eye, and Gordon had confirmed her vision—there was at least something else for her to grab hold of.

So she ran north, instinctively aware of direction even inside the hotel. When she heard doors crashing open somewhere far below, still she ran. She had stopped screaming now, because good sense told her she would not get very far that way. And she slowed her sprint to a jog; danger had come to visit, and she might need all her energy to escape.

*Your brother is alive north of here . . .*

"Andrew," she muttered, "I'm coming to find you."

She was leaving her friends behind, but already their memories were growing distant. They were like old dreams fading away, while new nightmares became her whole life.

She descended a staircase, having to slip through a landing door and wait in a deserted corridor when she heard people coming up. They passed her by, scurrying up a few more flights, and the threat they exuded was palpable. Continuing on her way, she reached the ground floor and ran north again, entering the kitchens and pausing for a while by a fire exit.

Motionless, her parents' dead faces flashed at her again.

"No!" She had to run. Had to move, never grow still, never stop until she and Andrew were together again, because he was all she had left in the—

From deep within the hotel she heard the sound of gunfire.

Lucy-Anne burst through the fire-exit doors into blazing sunlight, and the streets of the Toxic City resounded to the sound of her footfalls.

The Chopper soldier who had come through the door was kneeling, trying to turn his machine gun in the confined space. The one standing in the doorway behind him was far enough back to be able to aim properly, and they were his bullets that struck Gordon in the face and chest. The Irregular fell sideways and tumbled down the stairs.

Jack had only ever seen people killed on grainy internet images, and it was nothing like this. He heard Gordon's death, smelled it, tasted it as blood splashed the air and landed warmly across his face. He opened his mouth to shout, his voice adding to Emily's cry of horror.

Something blurred above his shoulder; Puppeteer's hand. His fingers flexed, knuckles seeming to ripple beneath the skin, and the kneeling soldier was snapped upright into his companion's line of fire.

Jack saw his second real-life death in the space of two seconds.

The standing soldier stepped back from what he had done, and the door swung shut until it rested against the fallen Chopper's hip.

Scryer, having dropped onto her stomach as soon as the door opened, threw herself across the dead soldier and fired a pistol through the half-open door. Jack heard a grunt and the sound of something hitting the carpeted floor beyond.

He turned around and looked up to the half-landing between floors 4 and 5. Sparky and Jenna were huddled there, pressed back against the wall, and Sparky's faced was dusted with plaster from where bullets had taken chunks from the masonry inches above his head. His eyes were wide with shock, but Jack could see that he was still alert.

Scryer crawled over the dead soldier, peered briefly into the fourth floor corridor, then ducked back into the stairwell. "More coming." A burst of gunfire confirmed her statement.

"Why are they doing this?" Rosemary hissed. She was looking down at Gordon, angry rather than shocked, and Jack wondered just how many people she had seen killed. If they got away from this he would ask her. If they got away, there were *many* things he had to ask.

"Us," Puppeteer said. He seemed to be agonising over something, staring at Jack and Emily and blinking rapidly. Then he bent down, snatched up the dead soldier's machine gun and offered it to Rosemary. "Take them down. We'll distract the Choppers. They probably don't even know you're here, so—"

Scryer fired into the corridor, ducking back and forth from behind the wall to loose two rounds each time.

"They might be coming up!" Rosemary said, pointing down the stairwell.

"That's why I'm giving you a machine gun." He pushed the weapon at her and she took it. The tall man stepped past her and drew a pistol from a holster beneath his jacket.

Someone shouted from far away, someone else responded, and an object bounced through the door.

"Stun grenade!" Scryer said. "Cover your ears, open your mouths!" She kicked out at the grenade. It skittered across the landing, slipping beneath the stair railing and falling down the stairwell. Seconds later it exploded.

Jack had never heard anything so loud. The blast wave punched his head, his ears, his eyes, and for a moment afterwards all he could hear was his heartbeat, muffled and fast with the fear pumping through him. Then, with a whine, the sounds from around him came in again, shouting and shooting and someone calling his name over and over again. He opened his eyes and Sparky was there, not more than a hand's breadth from his face but his voice coming from miles away. Behind him Emily was sitting on a stair, slowly unravelling the carry strap of her camera, looking into the lens, checking every setting methodically as though their survival depended on it.

That brought Jack around, more than Sparky shouting into his face and slapping his cheeks. Emily was in shock, and he had to look after her. He crawled to his sister, grabbed her arm and pulled her quickly past the half-open door. Scryer was still there shooting into the corridor beyond, and Puppeteer watched them go.

There was so much that Jack did not understand. One minute the Superiors were treating him and his friends as less deserving than animals, now they were fighting Choppers to give them a chance at escape. He was certain it was not simply a case of "the enemy of my enemy is my friend." It had something to do with their father, and the person called Reaper, and from what Rosemary had said back in that room . . .

They were one and the same.

Rosemary was already heading down towards the third floor. She carried the machine gun like a baby, and Jack had serious doubts about whether she'd even be able to use it. But the most he'd ever fired was an air rifle when he was younger, and his head was still ringing from the stun grenade.

They passed Gordon, and they could not help stepping in his blood.

"Faster!" Sparky shouted. "Have to go faster!"

Gunfire, shouting, the stink of violence, Emily coming along behind him, seemingly back to reality now but still frighteningly blank-faced; Sparky and Jenna behind her; the tang of Gordon's blood on his tongue; a scream from above, androgynous in its pain . . . and they passed the third floor access door without pause.

Rosemary was setting a fast pace for an older lady, and Jack could not help being impressed. But her fear was obvious, and it transferred easily to him.

There was an explosion above them, and the stairwell sang with shrapnel. Something cold touched Jack's ear. Dust stung his face. He kept running, step after step, holding Emily's hand with the grim certainty that her survival depended upon it.

"Grenade!" someone shouted, and he heard the metallic clash of something bouncing from the stair railings.

Emily screeched and fell into him. He had no chance, tripping forward with his arms outstretched to break his fall. He struck Rosemary's back and she fell as well, striking the landing and twisting, rolling, and Jack was down with her, Emily clasping onto his back.

Clang . . . clang . . . the grenade still fell, and though he had no idea where it would explode, moving felt better than lying still.

Rosemary had found her feet and was starting down the staircase to the second floor, and Jack and Emily were following, when the explosion came. It did not seem as loud as the first, but it blew him against the wall, snatching Emily's hand from his and spinning the world around his head. He was being struck from all sides, battered and thumped and cut; falling, or being hit by debris, he was not sure. When he gasped in a huge breath it was laden with dust and smoke. He opened his eyes, saw nothing, and for a few seconds he was terrified that he had been struck blind. But then someone wiped a hand across his face and Jack saw the blood.

"Jack?" Emily said, leaning over him, crying. He smiled and she cried even harder, and he thought, *Do I really look that bad?* More blood ran into his eyes and this time he wiped it away himself.

His head hurt. Everything hurt.

There was more shooting from up above, but it seemed to be receding.

Someone was shouting—Sparky—and the words faded in as if he was rushing in from a great distance.

". . . outside and meet you behind the hotel, find somewhere to hide?"

"Okay!" Rosemary called from much closer.

Jack sat up, and used the wall for support as he found his feet. Looking up, he realised how lucky he was to be alive. The whole flight of stairs they had just come down had collapsed, sending a shower of concrete, tiles and reinforcement rods tumbling below. On the landing above the gap, Sparky and Jenna were already peering cautiously through the door onto the third floor. Jack wanted to say something, but with a quick glance back at him, Jenna was through and gone. She looked terrified, and there was blood on her neck.

"Can you walk?" Rosemary asked him.

"Of course."

"Don't worry, dear," she said to Emily, "it looks worse than it is. Head wounds bleed a lot."

"Can you fix it?" the girl asked.

"Soon."

This time it was Emily leading Jack. They went down to the second floor landing, then had to climb carefully over the ruins of the fallen flight to head for the first floor.

"Where are the Superiors?" Jack asked.

"Still fighting, somewhere," Rosemary said. "But they're farther away. Must have pushed the Choppers back."

"So this is a normal day for you, I suppose?"

Rosemary surprised and delighted him by laughing. "This is the first time I've ever been shot at, would you believe? And I've never in my life fired a gun."

They passed the first floor door, and with every step Jack was feeling stronger. He used a handkerchief handed him by Emily to dab at the blood running down his forehead, and he even managed a smile when she briefly aimed the camera his way. *Glad that survived*, he thought, chuckling at how ridiculous that was. *Glad* we *survived!*

Jack tried to think tactics, but his mind was not working very well. Blown up, shot at, he was confused and disorientated. He could not recall what the street outside the hotel looked like, and for a few seconds he had trouble remembering whether it was even day or night. Then he remembered Gordon being shot—the blood splashing the air behind him, the way he'd fallen like a chunk of meat in an abattoir—and the present punched back at him.

"Won't they know we're in the stairwell?" he asked.

"Maybe," Rosemary said. She paused between first and ground floors, and for a terrible moment Jack thought she was going to hand him the gun. She shook her head. "It's all we can do. We can't afford to get trapped—"

The door a flight below them crashed open. It rebounded from the wall, and Jack heard the squeal as the mechanical door closer pulled it slowly shut again.

Silently, Rosemary signalled, *Up!*

They climbed back to the first floor landing. The door out of sight below them opened again, slower, and this time they heard footfalls as at least two people entered the stairwell, boots grinding on grit.

"Clear!" a voice whispered.

Jack opened the door, hoping against hope that the hinges on this one were better oiled. He glanced at the corridor beyond, then went through, pulling Emily after him. Rosemary followed, and he waited until she chose which way to go.

The corridor looked exactly like the one on the sixth floor, and that disorientated him even more.

He heard gunfire in the distance, then a muffled explosion that thudded through the building fabric and brought dust down from the ceiling. Rosemary paused, looking up, tilting her head to listen.

"Can you tell—" Jack asked, but then Rosemary clamped a hand across his mouth. She looked at Emily and nodded across the corridor at a door.

Emily had it open in an instant, and Rosemary pushed Jack in after her. It was a basic room, though still quite large, with two double beds, a desk, and an en-suite bathroom just inside the door.

Jack went immediately to the window, careful not to touch the heavy curtains as he peered outside. Emily came with him, and Rosemary remained at the door.

The window looked down behind the hotel, at an area once used for staff parking, deliveries, and service access. He could see no movement, but he concentrated on the areas where people could be hiding: behind the overturned bins; under the verdant bushes that had broken out from the neighbouring garden; inside the three vehicles still parked there, all sitting on flattened tyres and with unreadable graffiti daubed across their doors, bonnets, and roofs.

"What do you see?" Rosemary whispered. She was standing behind the closed door, one eye to the spy-hole.

"Nothing," Jack said. "Back of the hotel. No movement. They must have come in the front."

"They'll have it covered," she said. "They always . . ." She trailed off, and Jack watched her slowly raise her hand, then step back and point the gun at the door.

He motioned at Emily to lie between the two beds, then went to Rosemary, waiting for her to act. And then he heard the voices. They were distant at first, muffled and mysterious. But they were coming closer.

"Did you see them?" he whispered. Rosemary did not answer. She looked even more scared than she had before, and the gun in her hand was shaking.

"No," she said at last, "but I heard *him*."

"Him?"

"Miller."

"Who's—?"

Rosemary held up her head and nodded at the door.

The voices outside were louder now, and Jack started picking up some of the words. ". . . here somewhere, they must be, so I don't want any more . . ."

". . . every floor, from the bottom up." This was a quieter voice, obviously answering the man in command.

". . . stairwell . . . dead, and blood everywhere, so we must have hit one of them at least."

". . . more than a bullet to kill some of these freaks."

There was a pause at that, and Jack stepped closer to the door. They must be almost directly outside. He sensed Rosemary shifting so that she could still aim her gun at the wooden door, then he leaned over so that he could see from the spy hole.

Two men and a woman stood just along the corridor to the left, faces and bodies distorted by the door viewer. The tall man and the woman wore the distinctive blue uniforms worn by all Choppers, and they had guns held at the ready. The woman had short hair and soft features sharpened by her serious expression. The other man—shorter, older, black-clad, close-cropped grey hair the last stand against baldness—was obviously in charge. The way the other two looked at him . . . for a moment, Jack wondered if he was a Superior.

But these were Choppers, and if he had to hazard a guess, he'd name this short balding man as Miller. The name so feared by Rosemary.

"They're here somewhere," the short man said to the two soldiers. He looked at a small device in his hand, shook it angrily. "Not clear where, but *some*where. I want at least one of those two kids alive."

*Kids!* They'd been seen, or betrayed.

Rosemary glanced at him, eyes wide in surprise. Jack stepped away from the door, suddenly terrified that it would blow in, torn apart under a fusillade of bullets and smoke and chaos, and Rosemary would go down and the soldiers would come in, mindful of their order to keep *one* of the kids alive and deciding, on the spur of the moment, which one it would be.

"Yes, sir," the woman said. The other soldier mumbled an acknowledgement as well, and then Jack heard boots thudding away along the corridor.

*. . . at least one of those two kids . . .*

"Rosemary," he whispered, leaning in close.

"Not now," she breathed. "He's still out there."

Jack touched the woman's face and turned her until they were eye to eye. "You owe me."

Rosemary nodded, averting her eyes, then turned back to the spy hole.

Jack went to Emily, pulling her up to sit on one of the double beds. "We're okay," he said quietly, "we're safe." And he did not believe a word of it.

"They're trying to kill us," Emily said. "I saw that man, Gordon, and his head . . . his head . . ." She did not cry, did not sob, yet her words would not come.

"I know," Jack said. "But we're going to get out of here, I promise."

"And then we'll go and find Mum and Dad?"

"Yeah." He hugged his sister, and for the first time he thought of how finding their parents alive would change the relationship he and she had developed over the past two years. He hated the selfishness of that idea, and could barely understand it. But they had embarked upon this time of change eagerly, and perhaps now, when everything he knew and loved was under dire threat, was the first time he had truly considered the effects such change would have.

He could still hear gunfire in the distance, and from somewhere far away another explosion vibrated through the building. A large pane of glass in the window cracked.

"He's gone along the corridor," Rosemary said. "Jack, a second?" She was waving Jack to her without taking her eye from the spy hole.

Emily squeezed his hand and nodded.

When he reached the woman, she was holding the gun down by her side. But she was still shaking. "Professor Miller," she said without any prompting. "He's the head Chopper, from what any of us can make out."

"He wants me and Emily."

"What makes you think—?"

"I'm not bloody stupid, Rosemary."

She sighed. "I know. I know that, dear."

"What does he want with us?"

"Will you trust me, Jack?" She touched his shoulder, squeezing slightly as though trying to force trust into him.

"After this? After everything you've kept from us: the dogs in the tunnels; the Superiors; whatever it is you know about my father?"

"Yes, after all this, I still need you to trust me. There's plenty you don't yet know, but . . . it'll take some explaining. And now isn't really—"

More gunfire, this time from closer by. A door opened and slammed, followed by another, and then someone screamed in agony. The screaming went on and on until another gunshot shut it off.

"I've never done this before," Rosemary said, nodding down at the gun. "I'm just an old woman, but I'm doing my very best for you, son. Now that it's all gone so wrong so quickly, I'm doing my *very* best. So please, until we get out of here and find somewhere safe to talk . . . trust me?"

She was pleading. She tried not to make it sound like that, but it was obvious.

Jack nodded. "Okay. But everything I do in here, and every decision I make, is for the good of my sister."

Rosemary smiled and squeezed his shoulder again. "You're a good man, Jack."

*Man.* No one had ever called him that before. No one but himself.

When they opened the door, all was silent. They crept out into the hallway, Rosemary going first with her gun, and the building sat around them calm and still. They moved quickly along the corridor. It wasn't until they were closing on the fire exit door at the end that the shooting began.

Jack dropped, turning as he did so to fall across Emily. Rosemary fell against the wall and slid down to the floor, and for a terrible moment Jack thought she'd been hit. He looked for blood, but saw none, and then she turned around, looking past him back the way they had come.

She sighed. "Not this floor."

Jack shook his head. "This floor, but not this corridor. It's coming from the other wing. We need to go."

They moved to the end of the corridor, passing doors that might not have been opened for the past two years. *Are there bodies?* Jack wondered. *A sad story of lonely death behind each door?* The hotel smelled musty, though not unpleasant, but he had no idea whether there would still be the smells of rot and decay after so long. He felt as though he were inhabiting two times: the here and now, with people chasing and shooting at them through a deserted building in the dead Toxic City; and the past, where people spent brief periods of their busy lives in a room in one of London's many hotels.

Rosemary reached the fire escape door first. She looked back past Jack and Emily again, but did not seem to see anything that alarmed her.

"I'll go first," she said. "After I know it's safe . . ." She trailed off, her eyes went wide, and she brought the gun up in two hands. It was pointing directly at Jack's stomach.

"Wait!" he said, but she was not looking at him.

This time it was Emily who pulled Jack down. He turned as he fell, looking back along the corridor at the two Choppers who had appeared at its junction with the hotel's central core. They were the same man and woman he had seen talking to Miller outside the room door.

Bullets ripped along the corridor, slicing into the plaster walls, blowing jagged splinters from door frames, filling their world with violence and noise once more.

Rosemary braced herself against the wall, then looked down at her gun, turning it this way and that.

"Safety?" Jack shouted, because he really had no idea either.

The shooting stopped. "That's them!" a voice hissed.

"Okay," the woman said. "Just get the old bitch." The two soldiers ran along the hallway, guns raised, and when the woman stopped and braced into a firing position, the male Chopper jerked to a halt and shot his companion in the leg.

She grunted and flopped to the carpeted floor, dropping her gun and rolling immediately onto her back.

The tall soldier seemed to be fighting with his weapon, yanking it this way and that as if someone invisibly was holding the barrel. He pointed it at the woman writhing on the floor before him, shaking his head and moaning, "No, no . . ."

A shape appeared behind him at the corridor junction. Puppeteer.

"*No!*" the soldier shouted, and he shot his friend again.

Jack turned away, but he still saw her head whip back, and blood splash across the floor and up the corridor walls.

"Come on," Rosemary said. She nodded briefly to Puppeteer, then pushed the fire exit door open.

Jack hustled Emily through first, following her and turning around. As Rosemary let go of the door and its closer pulled it shut, he saw Puppeteer approaching the remaining Chopper, right hand held out and fingers playing the air.

The soldier screamed as his feet left the floor and his head was crushed, slowly, against the elaborately corniced ceiling.

"Jack," Emily said, "I should have got that on film."

"Kids," Rosemary said. "So resilient."

Jack barked one loud, harsh laugh, and then followed Rosemary down the stairs.

"Safety catch," he said.

Rosemary shook her head. "Dear, I honestly don't know if I could ever shoot another human being."

"Even if they're trying to shoot you?" Emily asked.

They reached the ground floor and continued down to the basement level. There were no windows here, no viewing panels in the doors, and the stairwell was dark and functional. Jack took a small torch from his rucksack and lit their way.

"Something has to set us apart from them," the woman said. And though Jack was still angry with her, his respect for her doubled.

The hotel's basement corridor was illuminated by a few narrow, dirty windows at high level. They looked out past iron railings at the street before the hotel. Something was burning out there, and Jack thought it was one of the Choppers' trucks.

"What the hell are those two Superiors doing?" he asked. "How can they take on an army?"

"I doubt there were just two," Rosemary said. "And they have such powers, Jack! I know of a fire starter, a woman who can confuse senses so that she's almost invisible, and someone who can change the colour of things."

The sounds of fighting had ceased for now, but the air was heavy inside the hotel, as though people with death on their minds still stalked its corridors and searched its empty rooms.

"I hope Sparky and Jenna are okay," Emily said, voicing a fear which Jack had been harbouring since seeing them exit the stairwell. Jenna had been wounded, and he hoped that Sparky would be sensible; no heroics, and no revenge for his dead brother. Not yet.

"They'll be fine," he said.

"And Lucy-Anne," Emily added, but Jack could think of no easy way to respond to that.

"We should leave," Rosemary said. She was gasping for breath, but looked like she would never give up. "If your friends made it down this far, they'll be waiting for us behind the hotel."

The basement was warren of store rooms, cupboards and corridors ending at closed doors. The air was grimy and grey. Emily pulled a penlight from her rucksack and it complimented Jack's torch, giving them enough light to find their way to a set of doors to the outside.

"Wait," Jack whispered. He held out his hands for the gun.

"Jack . . ." Emily said.

"Dear . . ."

"I'd rather shoot them and be damned, than be dead and morally superior," he said.

Rosemary handed him the weapon. He'd never fired a gun, but he knew the basics. He checked that the safety was off and held it in both hands, finger resting across the trigger and guard. It made him feel safer. It made him think he could do something to protect Emily, if he really had to.

He remembered Gordon's head flipping back as the bullets took his face apart.

He thought of the soldier he'd just seen shot, the blood and other stuff splashing from her shattered skull.

Slowly, he nudged the door. It was unlocked. It creaked open into the courtyard he'd seen from the hotel room. *They could be hiding anywhere*, he thought. *Ready to take us to Miller, just me and Emily*. The fact that the Chopper had said he wanted at least one of them alive did not make him feel the slightest bit safer.

He listened for Lucy-Anne; crying, shouting, screaming. She was not there.

They heard more shooting. It seemed to come from the front of the hotel, the shots echoing from abandoned buildings and giving them voice for the first time in years. There were shouts, yet more gunfire, and then a heavy *whump* as something exploded.

"Jack!" Sparky said. He appeared from behind one of the cars, and Jack almost did not recognise him. His denim jacket was darkened with blood, his hands red with it, and the look on his face was that of a child. *I'm scared*, it said. *None of this is happening . . . none of this is real . . . take me home . . .*

"Sparky! Where's . . . ?" But Sparky had already turned and looked down behind the car.

"Oh, shit," Jack said. He ran across the courtyard, nursing the gun across his chest as he went.

"Jenna?" Emily called. Jack heard her following him, and he hoped that she had put her camera away, because some moments were meant to be private.

Jenna was on the ground behind the car. It was an old Mazda 6, Jack saw, with one of those fish badges on the back that signified the owner was a Christian. *Wonder if it did them any good?* he thought, because Jenna was a believer too, he knew. And there she was, dying in a pool of her own blood.

She'd been shot in the stomach. Her hands were pressed there now, as if trying to penetrate to remove the foreign object. She could not lie still; her legs were raised and tensed, her shoulders lifting and falling alternately, and even though her eyes were open, Jack was not sure she could see him. She was in an awful amount of pain, biting her lower lip until it bled to prevent herself from crying out.

"Jenna." He knelt beside her and leaned over, trying to catch her eye. She saw him, and he knew that she saw. But she was doing something far more difficult than trying to communicate. Every breath she had, every shred of strength, was spent trying to keep herself alive.

"What happened?" Jack asked Sparky when his friend knelt next to him.

"We'd made it down to the ground floor. Stupidly thought we should run across the foyer." Every word was a gasp. "Someone was waiting behind the desk. Started shooting. She . . . fell. I dragged her into a doorway, down some steps, then I heard more shooting from up above. Screams. Whoever shot at us didn't follow us down. That's it. Been trying to stop the bleeding, but . . ." He shook his head. "You seen Lucy-Anne?"

"No," Jack said. "Rosemary!"

"Is the bullet still in there?" She stood behind them. Emily was beside her, trying not to look at the blood but unable to look anywhere else.

"Don't know," Sparky said.

"Why?" Jack asked.

"If it is, I can't do anything. Can't—"

"Don't tell me you can't!" Jack stood, cringing at his raised voice but unable to help himself. "After everything, *don't* tell me that!"

"If it's still in there and I heal the wound, it'll do no good. I can't take bullets out of people, Jack. But—"

"Can't you make her better?" Emily asked.

"If the bullet's gone through, then yes, dear, I can. If not, and I heal it inside, she'll probably develop an infection and die."

"Sparky," Jack said. "Help me." He searched around on the ground, shifting old leaves aside and picking up a fallen branch from one of the neighbouring garden's trees. He snapped a short section from it, eight inches long.

"What are you doing?" Sparky said.

"Seeing if the bullet came out the other side." He pressed the stick to Jenna's lips, and her mouth opened, teeth biting into the wood. She knew what he was doing.

"Not here," Rosemary said. "It's too dangerous!"

"Have your bloody gun back." Jack lobbed the weapon at her

and she caught it, uttering a startled cry. She turned to look up at the tall face of the hotel behind them.

"On three," Jack said. "One . . . two . . . three." He pushed Jenna up by the arm, Sparky pulled one of her legs, and as she turned onto her side she screamed into the wood, biting down hard enough to crack it and send splinters and shreds of bark spitting out.

Jack looked. Her jacket and shirt were soaked with blood all the way around. He lifted them up, exposing her bare back, and used her shirt to wipe across her skin. The blood smeared and smudged, but he found no exit wound there, and no sign that anything had broken the skin.

He hated doing this to his friend. He could see Emily's expression as she watched, and he hated what all this was doing to her, as well. It had gone so wrong so quickly that he could not imagine things ever being right again.

The wood snapped in Jenna's mouth and she screamed, unable to hold it in any longer.

Sparky was in front of her. He looked down at her stomach, turned away, and vomited.

"Not here!" Rosemary said. "We have to take her away, I know someone who might help, but *not here*!"

Jack leaned across Jenna to see why Sparky had puked, and her wound was pouting, something that could only have been her intestine protruding through the rip in her flesh. He closed his eyes and swallowed his bile, looking up at Emily. Wide-eyed, blinking slowly, pale, he suddenly saw himself in her, courage and love mirrored.

"Help me," he said, and his nine-year-old sister came to him without question, helping him pull Jenna's shirt tight across her stomach. Jack undid and unthreaded his belt, then tied it around Jenna. He had no idea whether he was doing the right thing. Rosemary, the healer, was looking the other way, and he hated her right then.

"Who can help?" Jack asked. He wanted to shout, but he could hear voices coming from somewhere far away, or echoing from close by.

"We need to get away," Rosemary said. A helicopter buzzed overhead, streaking across the hotel. Another one was coming in from the distance, and Rosemary was actually pacing back and forth. "Now!" she said. "We have to leave *now*! They'll be bringing reinforcements, and we'll *never* get away in one piece if that happens."

"One piece?" Sparky said, spittle hanging from his chin.

Rosemary looked down at Jenna. "She *can* still be helped," she said. "Trust me. If that wasn't the case, I'd be telling you to leave her where she is."

Between them, Jack and Sparky lifted the wounded girl. Mercifully she passed out, screaming herself into unconsciousness as Rosemary led the way along a narrow alley stinking of rot and filth, across a narrow street, and through a park where people had once sat to have lunch but which now was home to a band of noisy, angry monkeys.

The deeper they went into the Toxic City, the more Jack doubted they would ever find their way out again.

# CHAPTER TWELVE
# LAB RATS

> . . . although it's clear that this is a disaster the likes of which has never been seen before. London is effectively isolated, with no traffic entering or leaving. Reports of the death toll vary wildly, from a few hundred admitted by the British government, to several hundred thousand suggested by independent sources. A promised statement by the British prime minister has yet to materialize, and the questions have to be asked: What of the terrorists? Is the prime minister even still alive? And if he is, why has he not yet spoken to his people? In this time of global communication, it seems incredible that so little is being shared.
>
> —*CNN: Tragedy in London, 3:35 a.m. EST, July 29, 2019*

Lucy-Anne had forgotten her own name. But she knew the name of her brother.

"Andrew," she muttered as he ran north. The word worked like a talisman, parting the air before her and thickening it behind, drawing her ever-forward towards its owner. "Andrew," she said, and London heard the name. Thousands of fat pigeons watched her go by, and a parade of cats paused in the middle of a wide, vehicle-strewn road to sit and observe this strange sight.

The sounds behind her had ceased. *Everything* behind her had ended, because that was a place far in the past. Even her nightmare of dead parents . . . a memory, fading like a photograph left out in the sun.

Forward was the only place that existed now.

*Your brother is alive north of here*, she heard. She could not remember the voice or who owned it, but the words were her fuel. She would need food and water soon—her throat was parched, her sight blurry—but while there was still daylight in the sky, she could not waste any time.

She passed a place where a battle had taken place. Several trucks had been parked in a rough square, and their bodywork was pocked with hundreds of bullet holes. A couple of the trucks had burned, and their pale grey skeletons had rusted. Birds sat on the twisted metal, and something large moved ponderously in the cab of one of the unburned vehicles. She had no reason to stop and see what it was, because it was not her brother.

"Andrew," she gasped, and the word drew her on.

With every step, she lost more of herself. And every step made her past seem like a darker, older place.

They followed Rosemary, carrying the wounded girl between them. Jenna was in and out of consciousness, groaning, moaning from the pain. Jack wanted to check on her wound, but he feared that if they stopped they would never get going again. The strength had been knocked from them. Sparky looked beaten and pale, tired and shocked. Jack thought he seemed smaller than before, as though confirmation of his loss and what they had been through had lessened him somehow.

"Sparky," he kept saying, just to hear his friend's name and hoping to see the familiar confident, cheeky smile in response. But Sparky's reply was always slow, and weaker by the minute.

Emily walked beside Rosemary. She seemed to be handling things better than any of them.

They dodged from street to alley, square to park, and with every step they took the sounds of conflict receded. At one point they passed an area that seemed to have been flattened by bombing, and Jack asked Rosemary whether what had just happened was a regular occurrence.

"London suffers," is all she offered in response. "We're almost there." She went ahead, carrying the gun awkwardly and approaching the front door of an innocuous house in an unremarkable street. She lifted a plant pot containing the skeletal remains of a rose bush, picked up a key and opened the door.

"Is this where he lives?" Jack asked.

"I need to go and fetch him, and I'll be faster on my own." She glanced at Jenna. "And you two can't carry her much further. She's losing a lot of blood."

They went inside. The living room had a wide window looking out onto the wild back garden, and they laid Jenna on the sofa. She stirred, groaned, and then relaxed again. Her face was pale and sweat soaked her hair into thick, dark strands.

"Pain killers in the kitchen cupboard," Rosemary said. "Don't unlock the front door to *anyone* but me. If there's a knock, or any sign of the Choppers, get out the back door and run as fast as you can. Key's in the lock. There's a gate at the bottom of the garden, and—"

"We can't run anywhere with her," Sparky said.

"No, you can't." Rosemary looked grim, and Sparky stepped forward, about to vent his fury. Jack was pleased to see the old Sparky back again.

"We're not going anywhere," Jack said. "Just find this person you say can help."

"His name's Ruben," Rosemary said. "And I'll be back with him soon." She left the room and strode for the front door, gun slung over one shoulder like a novelty handbag. Jack followed her and grabbed her arm.

"The Superiors," he said. "My mother. My father. You need to tell me now."

"There's no time."

*"Please!"*

She was holding the front door handle, ready to open it and go out into this dangerous new world once again. She looked exhausted.

"What if you're caught?" he asked. "What if you're killed?"

"I can't explain everything right now, Jack, and if I tell you some of it, you'll want it all."

"They're alive," he said, a statement more than a question.

"Yes. Your mother's a healer, similar to me." She smiled. "I know her well. She lives in a makeshift hospital deep in an old Tube station. Susan's a good woman, Jack, and she talks about you and Emily so much that . . . I almost feel as if I've known you forever."

He closed his eyes and tried to recall a memory of his mother from before Doomsday. But he could not. He could only imagine her thin and pale, wasted and in despair, that tatty photograph in his back pocket come to life.

"And Reaper?" he said, looking at Rosemary again. "My father?"

"Your father," she nodded. "Jack—"

"Please, just tell me the basics." He kept his voice down because he did not want Emily hearing any painful truths, not yet. Not so soon after seeing people killed. And not from anyone but him.

"The Superiors are Irregulars who have utterly embraced their powers." Rosemary sighed. "They shun everyone else, spurn humanity, and see themselves as the future. They set themselves apart. As you've seen, they can be brutal, and they're driven. There are those who say they have plans—escape, domination, control—but that their powers haven't yet developed enough to implement them." She looked down at her feet.

"And?"

"And Reaper is their leader."

*Leader?* He blinked, trying to imagine his father—softly

spoken, tall, and loving—resembling Puppeteer in manner or intent. "What can he do?"

"He kills people with his voice."

"He's *killed* people? What does—"

"I told you there's no time right now! Jenna needs help, and soon. Let me go, Jack. *Please*."

He lowered his head. Without another word, and without a backward glance, Rosemary left. Jack wondered what she felt most: guilt, or relief.

Back in the living room, Emily and Sparky glanced up when he entered, and perhaps they read something else in his grave expression.

"Is Jenna going to die?" Emily asked.

"No!" Sparky said, and he had truly returned, Jack's angry, wonderful friend. "No, she isn't! Not on my bloody watch." He sat next to Jenna on the sofa and took her hand. "You die, you'll have me to answer to." Only death would make him let go.

Jack shook his head. "Rosemary's going to do her best," he said. And though there was so much more to tell, he did not have the energy to do so right then.

"I'm hungry," Emily said, and Jack realised that he was as well. However ridiculous that it may have seemed after what they had been through, and what they had seen, hunger gnawed at his stomach. He looked at Jenna's constant pained movements, her blood, her pale face, and he left the room to find the kitchen.

Jack felt dizzy. He leaned against the worktop and pressed his hands to the surface, casting prints in dust. Breathing deeply, he closed his eyes and tried to see past what had happened. But all he could see was red. *It's much worse than we ever thought it could be*, he thought. *So much worse.*

"Is it a war?" Emily said quietly. She'd crept in behind him, and Jack turned and hugged her to him, resting his chin on top of her head.

"I think so," he said. "And I'm not sure anymore that we've done the right thing. Jenna might be . . ." He gasped, unable to say the word. "And Lucy-Anne's gone, none of us know where, none of us have *any idea* what's happened to her, who's got her, where she is . . ." He cursed, and this time it was Emily's turn to hold him. "I just can't believe it's all gone so bad like this!" he growled, and every word hammered the guilt deeper.

"It's not your fault," Emily said. "It's *their* fault." *Them, they, their*, he and his friends had used those words so much to signify the devious government and military that perpetuated the myth of a dead, toxic London, and Jack had never been sure that Emily knew exactly who or what *they* were. Now he *was* sure, and he felt ashamed at ever doubting her.

"I don't want any more people to die," he said.

"Mum and Dad?" Emily asked quietly.

"They're alive, Emily."

She pulled back and looked him in the eye, picking up on his hesitation. "Rosemary told you?"

"Yeah. Mum's a healer, like her."

"And Dad?" she asked, his beautiful little sister, wide-eyed and confused.

"Alive, but she doesn't know him." He couldn't tell her yet. There was so much he didn't even know himself.

"Then that's good, isn't it?"

"Yeah, Ems, it's good."

"Don't call me Ems, Tobes."

"Whatcha gonna do about it?"

Emily hugged him again, and they stood together in the kitchen of a dead stranger's house.

They looked around for some food, but there was nothing here to eat. If Rosemary and some of her friends used this as a safe house, they certainly didn't keep it stocked. They did find some bottled water, however, and they all swigged down most of a bottle each. Sparky gently lifted Jenna's head, while Emily poured some into her mouth, but it dribbled out when she winced in pain, soaking her neck and the sofa beneath her.

"We can't let this happen," Sparky said. "It's not fair."

"Rosemary will do her best," Jack said.

"*We* need to do our best, too. We've lost Lucy-Anne, Jack. We just let her go, get lost, and we *left* her back there."

"We didn't have a choice." He could see that Sparky understood, but Jack felt impotent and helpless. "You do know that, don't you? We could have—"

"She could be dead, Jack."

"We could have *all* been killed in there, and no one would ever know."

"Yeah," Sparky sighed. "No one's ever going to know about Stephen. How he died, where. Why. Even Mum and Dad won't give a shit, if I ever get out and manage to tell them. They won't believe me, or they won't care. He died much longer ago for them than for me."

"He knew you were a good brother, mate."

"You think so?"

"Definitely." Jack sat in an armchair across from the sofa, looking at their dying friend.

"She won't be long," Emily said.

"She can't be." Sparky was still holding Jenna's hand.

They waited for three hours, and every minute was a lifetime. Jack and Emily used some of the bottled water to wash as best they could, but Sparky refused to leave Jenna's side. She woke up a few times, but she would sweat and moan and cry out, and they were all glad when the pain took her into unconsciousness again. It was better for her, and easier for them.

Jack was desperate to change his jeans. They were soaked with blood—Gordon's, Lucy-Anne's, and his own—and though mostly dried, he could still smell it. He rooted around upstairs and found a pair of jeans, dusty but whole, that were only one size too large for him. And it was while he was changing that he suddenly remembered the photograph.

It was soaked. Stained. Beyond repair. He wiped it, licking his fingers and smearing the blood across its surface, dabbing it on old bedding, but his mother's image was marked forever. He hoped it was not an omen.

He slid the photo into the rump pocket of his new jeans and went back downstairs.

They talked about Lucy-Anne. Jack was struck with guilt for leaving her behind, but they all agreed that they'd had no real choice. Events had carried them along. They discussed what could have happened to her, and perhaps with Jenna as she was they found it necessary to be honest with each other, and themselves. *Maybe she was caught*, Sparky said. *She might be dead*, Emily whispered. Jack nodded at them both, remembering the sounds of chaos and conflict echoing from the hotel even as they fled. And what he had heard the Chopper, Miller, saying to his soldiers gave him little hope.

When they heard the front door opening and the sounds of people entering, carefully and cautiously, Jack leapt for the living room door, ready to slam it in the intruders' faces.

"It's me," Rosemary said, and Jack slumped with relief.

She entered the room with a short fat man, his face resembling a nervous rat's. His skin was slick with sweat, and he stared around at them as though they were exhibits, not people. His gazed rested on Jenna, and without a word he sat on the sofa beside her and gently lifted her hands from her wound.

"This is Ruben," Rosemary said. He lifted one hand in acknowledgement, never taking his eyes from Jenna's stomach.

"Can you help her?" Sparky asked.

"Yes. You'll need to give me some room, though."

"Do you need anything?" Emily asked. "Water, something to wash your hands?"

"No," he said. He rolled up his sleeves and entwined his fingers, and Jack saw for the first time how large and fat his hands were, with fingers like swollen sausages. After cracking his knuckles he glanced at Rosemary, then the others.

"Keep away," Rosemary said. "You can watch, but don't interrupt him while he's operating. It's dangerous."

"Operating?" Sparky stood from the sofa, relinquishing his hold on Jenna's hand with some reluctance. "He doesn't have any knives, or anything."

Ruben smiled, held up his hands and waggled his fingers. Then he went to work.

Jack could not help watching, fascinated as well as disgusted. Emily stood beside him filming the whole thing, and once again he marvelled at her toughness.

Ruben's obesity and fat fingers belied his grace and deftness of touch. He felt around the wound first, using a soft yellow cloth from his pocket to wipe away the blood so that he could see the hole more clearly. His fingers trailed across the skin, barely touching, and Jack saw Jenna's stomach twitch as though tickled. Then he pressed slightly harder, flexing the skin and pushing down around the wound. Rosemary had not told any of them exactly what Ruben's gift was, and Jack was unsure of what to expect.

Ruben pushed his fingers into Jenna's stomach.

Jack gasped and stepped forward, but Rosemary reached out and grabbed his arm, shaking her head. She mouthed the word *No*, and held on until Jack nodded and stepped away again.

Initially it looked as though Ruben's fingers were pressed into the wound, following the route of the bullet through Jenna's guts and towards her spine. But then Jack realised that the big man's fingers had punctured the skin around the wound, though no fresh blood flowed, and Jenna seemed to be in no more discomfort than before. The bullet hole pouted and seeped a fresh flow of blood and clear fluid, and the purplish curve of her intestine once again showed at the rip.

Ruben was concentrating so hard that sweat speckled his balding head, soaked the back of his shirt and dripped from his nose and chin. When it mixed with Jenna's blood he seemed unconcerned, and Jack started to worry about infection, the germs on his hands, and—

*He's stuck his bloody hands into her gut!*

He glanced across at Sparky and saw that the boy was astounded.

Ruben lifted himself up slightly, hunching over Jenna before pushing deeper. Both of his hands were in her stomach now, her light skin stretched tight against Ruben's darker skin, and Jack could barely see the join. The man's hands worked inside her, tendons flexed on his wrists, and the muscles in his forearms performed their own complex, delicate dance as he probed deeper, and wider.

Jenna groaned, still unconscious, and tried to press her hands back against her wound.

"Hold her hands, please," Ruben said. Sparky and Emily went to the sofa and did as he asked, stroking Jenna's skin and unable to look away. Emily still bore the camera in her other hand, training it on Ruben, the wound, Jenna's face, and then turning slightly to record Jack's reaction as well.

"There it is," the man said, his voice barely a whisper. "Now then . . ." He leaned closer, more sweat dripping from his face, and Jack saw that his eyes were closed. He was operating by touch alone.

Jenna groaned and said something, too distorted by pain for Jack to make sense of.

"It's okay, girl," Ruben said softly. "Almost done, almost out, and then the lady Rosemary will do her work."

"Have you got it yet?" Sparky said, and Rosemary threw a stern look his way.

Ruben surprised them all with sudden movement, tugging his hands from Jenna's stomach, flinging them up above his head and speckling the ceiling with rosettes of blood. Something bounced from the wall and fell behind the sofa. The fat man tried to stand but he seemed weak, and instead he slipped from the sofa and sat on the floor, breathing heavily. "It's out," he said.

Jack rushed to Jenna, kneeling beside Sparky and Emily and looking at her wounded stomach. The tear from the bullet was still obvious and horrific, but there were no other wounds to show where Ruben's hands had entered.

Ruben was looking at his hands, gently dabbing the smears of blood that speckled them like liver spots. There was nowhere near as much as there should have been.

"Where's the bullet?" Sparky asked. He crawled around the end of the sofa and looked behind it, stretching his arm into the gap between sofa and wall. "Bloody hell," he muttered, standing with the prize in his hand. The bullet was half the size of his thumb, squashed and distorted by the impact on Jenna's flesh.

"Move aside, please," Rosemary said. She nudged past Jack, waited while Ruben crawled across the floor, and knelt beside Jenna.

The girl screamed, hands pressing down onto her wound once more.

Rosemary put her hands on Jenna's stomach, grew very still, and her face went blank.

"That was incredible!" Sparky said. He'd hardly left Jenna's side since Rosemary had healed the wound, and now he sat at one end of the sofa with the girl's head in his lap. She seemed to be asleep now rather than unconscious, and she had already stopped moaning from the pain. "She was dying in front of us, and now . . ." He shook his head.

"It's just what we can do," Rosemary said, but she was smiling.

"It's a miracle! No bloody wonder the Choppers are hunting you all."

"Yes, well, I'd rather not be hunted," Ruben said.

"They told us you were all monsters," Emily whispered. "They showed pictures on the telly and the Internet. Pictures of . . . *monsters*."

Ruben smiled and motioned for Emily to go to him. She sat beside him on the other, smaller sofa in the room.

"Do I look like a monster to you?" he asked.

"Of course not. You look like my friend Olivia's dad."

Jack laughed, and Ruben honoured him with a smile as well.

"And is Olivia's father a monster?"

"No," Emily said. "Though he's a bit gruff sometimes. And he smells of smoke." She frowned. "I've always known they were lying, because Jack made sure I did. But they still tell everyone else that anyone left alive in London is a mutant. Dangerous."

"Some are," Ruben said, smiling ruefully. "Some are."

"They met some Superiors back at the hotel," Rosemary said.

"But they helped us," Jack protested. "If it weren't for them . . ." He thought of Lucy-Anne, and the guilt cut in again, harsh and sharp. *Is there someone that can heal me of this?* he wondered, and he thought there probably was. But some things needed to be suffered.

"And if the Choppers hadn't turned up," Rosemary said, "there's no saying what Puppeteer and Scryer would have done to us."

"Maybe Lucy-Anne is with them!" Emily said. "Maybe they rescued her, and—"

"If they had, they'd have let her go again," Ruben said. "Even we're looked down upon by them, but you . . ."

"We're normal," Emily said.

"My girl," Ruben said, "I'll tell you something, and whether or not your brother or friends agree, you listen to me because I know: there's no such thing as normal."

"So maybe she went north to look for her brother?" she said.

"She's dead," Sparky said. "She was mad, grief-stricken, no way she'd have come to her senses quick enough to hide or get out. No way."

"We can't know that for sure," Jack muttered, but a voice inside was whispering *we can, we know, we're sure.* He turned to Rosemary. "How safe are we here?"

"As safe as anywhere," Rosemary said. "We use a house a couple of times, then abandon it. I hid here for a week a few months ago when the Choppers did a sweep through this part of town."

Ruben grunted. "They took Horace, Pat, and Bethany, that time."

"So, yes, it's safe," Rosemary said, sighing sadly. "I think we should stay here tonight, give Jenna a chance to get her strength back."

"But you've cured her," Emily said. "Why can't we just go and find Lucy-Anne, then look for my mum and dad."

Rosemary and Ruben swapped glances, and Jack saw their loaded look.

"What?" he asked.

"I've cured her, but she's tired from what she's been through," Ruben said. "She needs a rest."

"Not that," Jack said. "There's something else, isn't there?"

"Your parents," Ruben said. "Rosemary told me who you are, though I wasn't aware she'd gone out to get you."

"Do you really want her to hear this?" Rosemary said, nodding at Emily.

Jack went to say something, but Emily beat him to it. "I'm older than I look." She stood, left the sofa, and sat beside Jack on the floor.

"Okay then," the healer said. "But you're not going to like it."

"Tell me something new," Jack said.

Sparky laughed softly. "The world's gone to shit."

Rosemary started talking.

She told them all about Reaper. Emily glared at Jack.

"She only mentioned it just before she went," he said. "I'd have told you."

Her glare softened. "He's alive. Anything else doesn't really matter right now."

"I'm afraid it *does* matter," Ruben said. "Reaper is like those Superiors you met at the hotel, only much worse. He barely acknowledges that we exist, and as for outsiders . . . I've no idea how he'll react. He might just kill you, I suppose."

"But he's our father," Jack said.

Rosemary shook her head slowly. "Jack, Emily, his time as your father ended two years ago. The virus Evolve altered his mind, just as it altered the minds of everyone else in London it didn't kill. But with him and the Superiors, it changed so much more. He's a different man now. He'll know you, perhaps, but that might not mean anything. Although we hope . . ." She trailed off and looked across at Jenna, lying peacefully asleep with her head resting on Sparky's thigh.

"You never came looking for her dad, did you?" Jack asked. "You obviously knew about what he'd done, and what he'd had done to him. But you came looking for me and Emily."

"Yes," Rosemary said. "Because of Reaper, and because of what you might be able to make him do."

"But you're telling me I can't make him do anything! He'll barely know us, that's the impression you're giving. What the hell am I supposed to do?"

"He's my daddy," Emily said, and Jack could see that the raised voices were upsetting her. But this was something that he could not leave alone: another lie, another deception, and now he needed to know the truth. Lucy-Anne was gone, Jenna had almost been killed, and the time for being blind was over.

"We're desperate," Ruben said, and the fat man looked suddenly vulnerable and hopeless. "The Choppers pick us off the streets one by one, take us away, and cut us up to . . . to look for what makes us what we are. We're just lab rats to them, not humans. Sometimes they capture a Superior, but usually it's us Irregulars."

"Because the Superiors put up more of a fight?" Jack asked.

"Yes, because they're able to," Rosemary said. "Many of us have powers that are benevolent by their very nature. Mine, Ruben's. But the Superiors . . . well, you've seen what some of them can do. And there are more."

"So *have* you tried to hook up with them?" Sparky asked. It seemed so obvious to him. "Join forces to take on the Choppers? From what I've seen round here so far, you lot just hide out in little groups or alone, sneak around at night like bloody rats trying not to get trapped. Get active, not passive."

"We tried fighting back on our own, first of all," Ruben said. "Six months after Doomsday, all of us still trying to come to terms with what had happened to London, what had happened, and was still happening to us—"

"Still happening?" Jack cut in.

"Our talents are getting stronger all the time," Rosemary said.

"And that's scaring them. Their efforts to capture us are speeding up, and sometimes becoming more desperate."

"So there we were," Ruben continued, "cut off from the outside world, many of us separated from families outside or . . . bereaved." He looked away, remembering someone Jack could never know.

"I'm sorry."

Ruben shrugged. "There's been so much loss that, in a way, personal grief is even more tragic. Anyway . . . we tried. A group of us got together, and when the Choppers next sent in their armoured column we attacked them. Fire bombs, a few guns we'd found lying around, homemade explosives. And Peter. Remember Peter?"

Rosemary smiled, and Jack could tell that more sadness was yet to come.

"Peter was a young boy, a couple of years younger than you, who could direct bursts of energy from his mind. It cooked electrical circuits, blew computer chips. He called it his Mind Blower. He helped us, trying to take out the armoured vehicles' navigational computers and communications. And it worked. But only until they shot him."

"The attack went on," Rosemary said, "and when they left we thought we'd driven them away."

"Until the next morning," Reuben whispered. "Gordon found him. You met Gordon. And I'm not sad that Gordon's gone now, because he never could really come to terms with what they'd done to Peter."

Rosemary glanced at Emily.

"She's my sister," Jack said. "She needs to know what we know."

"Okay," she said. "Gordon found Peter crucified on the front façade of Harrods. They'd used nail guns to pin him to the wall. Arms, legs, feet. Gordon was sure he must have still been alive when they did it, dying from his gunshot wound, because there was so much blood."

"They took his brain," Ruben said. "Cut off the top of his head and just . . . took it."

"A warning?" Sparky asked.

Ruben snorted. "Yes, right. Just to tell us how little we mean to them as living things, but as carriers of all these new gifts . . . we're priceless."

"So now most of us run, like you said, Sparky." Rosemary nodded. "We run, and we hide, alone or in small groups. Trying to avoid the Choppers because we know what they do with those of us they capture."

"You told me you wanted exposure," Jack said. "That if we came in, saw everything, took some pictures and film, we could go back out and blow it all wide open."

"There's no way they'd allow that," Ruben said.

"But we have to try!"

Rosemary shook her head. "They can cover up what's happened here from the rest of the world. They can hide the existence of the new talents created on Doomsday—an evolved humanity, how *incredible!*—and the fact that those talents are growing every day. They can do all that, and keep the rest of the country ignorant of the truth, so do you really think a few pictures and bits of film will be believed?"

"Get them to the right places, sure," Sparky said.

"Do you believe everything you see on TV?" Rosemary asked.

"'Course not. Load of bullshit."

"That's my point."

"But . . ." Jack shook his head, angered by the Irregulars' lack of faith and belief in what was right, but unable to see a way through. "There's hope," he said. "You have to hang onto that."

"I lost it long ago," Rosemary replied. "At least, until we found out about you. Because the only hope for the people left alive in

London—several thousand of us, perhaps—and the powers we have, is for all of us to unite and fight our way out."

Sparky laughed. "You're joking, right? Get together, you and all those Superior superhero wannabes, and start a war?"

"Not *start* a war," the woman replied. "*Finish* one."

"And can you give us any alternative?" Ruben asked.

"Not off the cuff, but I can tell you it'll end up with them killing you all," Sparky said.

"And you want me to go to my father, this Reaper you talk about, and persuade him to do this?" Jack asked.

"In a nutshell," Rosemary said. "We tried, and he turned us down. You're our last hope."

"But you don't believe he'll even care."

"Not anymore." She shook her head, wretched, tortured. "Our last hope is almost hopeless."

Jack sat back against the wall and sighed. He looked at the ceiling and saw a fine network of webs, and in the corner sat a small, fat spider. It was waiting for unwary flies to become caught in its net. And if a dozen flies ganged up on it, the result would simply be a fatter spider.

"So how did you find out about Jack and Emily?" Sparky asked. "Someone with a people radar? Some bloke who can sniff paternal genes across hundreds of miles?"

"No," Rosemary said, "their mother told me about them."

"My mother," Jack said, and he smiled. He thought of Sparky immediately and felt bad, but his friend was looking down at Jenna's face. Now that he knew his parents were still alive, the idea of exposing the lies of the Toxic City seemed even more pressing. Because if he had discovered they were alive only to lose them again—either to the Choppers, or if his father disowned them—Jack did not think he could mourn a second time.

"I need to see her first," he said. "You can take me down to where she is?"

"Tomorrow," Rosemary said, her face flushed. "So you'll do it? You'll go to Reaper?"

"I'll go to my father, yes. How will you find him?"

"He's not difficult to find."

"Then why don't the Choppers come and take him?" Emily asked.

"They've tried," Rosemary replied. "Often. None of them ever come back."

*My dad's a killer*, Jack thought, but the idea was not as reprehensible as it should have been. Perhaps in his mind, he was already viewing his father as a radically changed man. It had been two years, and when they met they would be strangers. Maybe that was the best way for whatever future there was between them to begin.

"Thank you," Ruben said, his gratitude heartfelt.

"And I'm sorry for . . ." Rosemary said, but she trailed off.

"All the lies?" Sparky suggested.

Jack laughed. "We're used to them. Didn't you know it's now lies that run the world?"

As the sun settled red across the London rooftops, they heard the sound of a wolf's howl in the distance.

"Is that really what I think it is?" Sparky asked.

"I saw one once," Rosemary said. She was sitting on the small sofa beside Ruben, eating tinned tomatoes from a large bowl. She'd fetched the food from a house further along the street, saying that keeping safe houses well stocked would take away the safety. "Hyde Park, about a year ago. That's a wild place now. The trees and bushes have gone mad, the grasses come up to your knees, and the first of the mass graves is there. Lots of it was dug up by wild dogs and other carrion things just after the authorities withdrew from London, so there are bones scattered everywhere. And I found somewhere where the bones had been arranged around a copse of trees like some sort of . . . symbol. I went closer to the bushes, and a wolf came out. It was beautiful. So powerful, so *of nature*, that I felt . . . insignificant. Here we are, humans being inhumane as we always have done, and the wolf survives." She nodded, staring at the wall opposite and seeing into her past.

"Wolves placed the bones?" Sparky asked.

"Maybe," she said. "Maybe not. I'm more inclined to think it was some sort of offering or worship of the pack."

"By people?"

"By people. There are some . . . you haven't met or seen any yet, but Jack, when I take you down to your mother you'll see some of the people she looks after. Mad. Worse than mad . . . an unnatural insanity, because what happened to us is entirely man-made. And some people haven't been able to handle the talents they've developed."

"And Mum heals them?"

"She looks after them. They can't be healed because there's nothing wrong with them. It's just that their bodies and minds can never accept the sudden change."

Jenna stirred. Everyone froze. She smacked her lips, and frowned. "Did someone put a dead rat in my mouth while I was sleeping?"

"Hey, Jenna!" Sparky squealed, leaning down and kissing her hard on the lips.

"Oh, gross," the girl said, but she smiled as she tried to push herself up on her elbows. Sparky helped, lifting her into a sitting position and placing a couple of cushions behind her back.

"Welcome to the land of the living!" Jack said without a trace of irony. "How do you feel?"

Jenna paled and her hands flew to her stomach. "I've been shot!"

"You're all better now," Emily said.

"Better?"

Jack nodded at Rosemary and Ruben, both smiling as the girl came around.

"Rosemary," she said. "Again. Thanks."

"Ruben took the bullet out," the woman said, nodding at the fat man beside her.

Sparky produced the bullet from his pocket. "Kept it for you. Maybe it'll make a nice pendant, or something."

Jenna frowned at the bullet as he dropped it in her hand. She looked around, confused, and her gaze settled on Sparky. "You *kissed* me?"

"Er . . . sorry," he said. "But if it makes you feel better, you're right. You tasted like dead rat."

"Where's Lucy-Anne?" Their silence was no real answer, so she asked again.

"We don't know for sure," Jack said. "She never came back."

"Where are we now?"

Rosemary filled her in on their flight from the hotel, through the streets to this place. She left out the discussion they'd had, leaving that for Jack.

"We have to go and look for her," Jenna said.

Jack shook his head. "It's too dangerous, and now it's getting dark—"

"She's our friend," Jenna said, her voice weak but firm. "She's your girlfriend, Jack. We can't just abandon her because she ran away."

"I've gone through all this," Jack said, and the guilt came in yet again.

"She could be lying injured somewhere. Shot, like me." She looked at Rosemary. "Do you know anyone that can find her?"

"Not now Gordon's dead," she replied. "But that doesn't mean there isn't anyone else."

"Then we all go and look, starting at—"

"It's impossible," Rosemary said. "If she'd stayed in or around the hotel, the Choppers would have her by now. If she ran further, then we have no clue as which *way* she ran. And it's not as if we can walk through the streets calling her name."

"So we just give up on her?"

Nobody answered for a while, until Emily went and sat beside Jenna. "I think she's gone to find her brother," she said. "Alive somewhere, in the north. In fact, I'm sure of it."

"How can you know?" Rosemary asked.

"Because that's what I'd have done." Emily grinned at Jack, and he smiled at his little sister.

"Maybe," Jenna said. "I hope so. It just feels so bad . . . so unfair. God, I need sleep." She slid down until her head rested against Sparky's shoulder. He froze, delighted, and she grinned, pushing his shoulder around as if fluffing up a pillow before closing her eyes.

Jack smiled. He'd wanted to see these two getting it together for a while. Sparky would be a challenge for anyone, but perhaps being attacked by dogs, chased by government soldiers, blown up, and shot in the stomach was all Jenna had needed.

"We all need sleep," Rosemary said. "It's been quite a day. There are two bedrooms upstairs. Ruben and I can sleep down here."

The mention of beds and sleep got them all yawning. Jack and Emily went up first. They used bottled water and toothpaste from Emily's backpack to clean their teeth, then they chose the twin room and closed the door. Emily fell asleep almost before her head hit her pillow, and Jack sat up for a while, staring at his little sister. *Tomorrow we're going to see Mum*, he thought. He was excited and afraid in equal measures.

He lay down, but was not surprised when he could not sleep. A rush of memories came back to him, good times with his parents that he had long forgotten, and he wallowed in them, smiling at some and crying softly at others. He'd never really known nostalgia as a powerful emotion, but he did now. Before today he'd laboured under the belief that things could, by some miracle, go back to normal. Find his mother and father, escape the Toxic City, go home, live together again as they had been more than two years before. But now he acknowledged the firm reality that his family had changed forever. Nostalgia, as he experienced it there in a stranger's bed, could not allow for things ever being the same again.

He heard the stairs creaking and Sparky and Jenna talking in subdued tones. They went into the double bedroom next door, and for a while he heard their voices, Sparky's low and deep, hers soft and sad. There were tears as well, and then talking again, and after a period of silence he heard the first gentle moans of pleasure. Sleep came to Jack at last, giving privacy to his friends.

# CHAPTER THIRTEEN
# ROOK

. . . . . . . . . . *static* . . . . . . . . . .

—*Reception on every UK radio and TV channel, 6:00–9:00 a.m. GMT, July 29, 2019*

Whatever had broken in Lucy-Anne's mind was trying to fix itself. She could feel it like an itch, a tickle so deep inside her that it could never be reached, and she shook her head now and then to try and dislodge it.

Her run slowed to a fast walk, and that was when she started to see people. The first was a face in a window, pale and sickly, and when she did a double-take the face was gone. There was no expression to read there at all, and she purposely got lost in a network of streets and alleys in case the person decided to follow.

North, ever northward, and between every blink she saw the faces of her parents from her nightmare.

*I'm never going to sleep again*, she thought. Though she was in this terrible place, it was the blank plane between sleeping and waking that horrified her now. There had been the dogs, though her memory of them had grown indistinct, and other memories were even vaguer, so distilled through whatever had snapped in her mind that she could not tell whether they were real events or dreams. Perhaps the distinction no longer mattered.

Lucy-Anne *knew* that something had snapped inside. Hers was a conscious madness, a waking breakdown, and when she dwelled on it her head hurt as though physically injured. North was all that mattered, because somewhere in that direction would be Andrew.

Someone walked into the street ahead of her. The figure paused, turned her way, froze.

Lucy-Anne ran between buildings, stumbling over a pile of refuse, ducking through gardens, rushing past a Tube station with a pile of skeletons wedged in its entrance gates. She hit a main road and quickly turned left, welcoming the shadows cast by the large buildings to her right. There she slowed, listening in case she had been followed but never willing to stop her forward momentum.

The first black shape passed behind her with the sound of a whisper in the night.

She spun around, skidding to a halt in the middle of the wide residential street. Her hands came up, but there was nothing there. She fumbled the knife from her pocket and held it out before her, but it felt pitiful against the world. There were tall four-storey buildings on one side. Behind her was an overgrown park at the centre of what must be a large square, and staggered along the road were cars. Many of them were still parked in an ordered row along the pavement. There were Porsches, BMWs, Mercedes, Bentleys, and the buildings stared at her with rich, dead eyes.

Something else fluttered behind her, and when she crouched and turned she saw a black shadow disappearing into the park. She frowned. Leaves rustled ten feet above the ground, and more shadows moved through the trees.

"Birds," she whispered. And as if conjured by her voice, they made themselves known.

They burst from the undergrowth in the park, lifted from rooftops and erupted from several broken windows in the building facades, darkening the air and swooping towards her without making a single sound.

The scream came from Lucy-Anne as she ran, because she had seen these rooks before.

She sprinted straight into one of the expensive cars, flipped across its bonnet and smacked her head against cool metal. As her vision faded, she heard a long, high whistle, and instead of retreating it seemed to grow louder as consciousness left her.

She is alone, in a ruined landscape of forgotten buildings and hopelessness, but she is at peace with her own company. She is walking through the streets without fear or trepidation. Sometimes she whistles, sometimes she sings, but she is just as comfortable with only the sound of her footsteps on dusty pavements. She would claim contentment—there are things undone, and fate hangs on a knife-edge somewhere away from where she is now—but for the moment, she is as happy as she can be.

And then she becomes aware of the others. They are crowding around her, though unseen. They stalk her across rooftops and in tunnels beneath the ground, crashing through from one terraced building to the next, and they only have eyes and ears for her.

She starts to hurry, hoping to outrun them. But that will be impossible. Not because they are fast and she is slow, or because they know this place far better than her. But because she is *making* these pursuers with every breath, every thought, and every time she sleeps they multiply many times over.

She breaks the silence and screams, because she knows that eventually they will catch her. And kill her.

She came to, opening her eyes a crack and immediately becoming disorientated at the movement. The sky had turned black, and it was swimming in circles above her.

The rooks screeched, hundreds of them, perhaps thousands, and she rolled over and covered her ears to shut out the sudden, terrifying sound. She screamed, but though she felt the cry vibrating in her throat, she could hear nothing.

Queasy, swaying, she stood and skirted around the parked car, heading for the gated front gardens. If she could only get into a house away from these things, then maybe . . .

The memory of this nightmare hit her and she turned, searching for the shadow she had seen. There was no one there. The rooks were descending closer, though, almost filling the sky as they shifted this way and that, waving and pulsing like a shoal of fish.

She crashed through a gate, ignoring the sting of nettles blooming out across the path as she ran to a front door. It was locked. She bashed on it and shouted, still unable to hear her own voice. But of course; everyone here was dead.

Almost *everyone!* she thought. *Andrew isn't dead. He's alive, somewhere to the north of here he's alive, and I'm going to—*

Something stroked across her cheek and she thrashed her arms, touching nothing. It was an intimate touch, almost a caress, and through the screeching of rooks and the alien flapping of their wings, Lucy-Anne heard a soft, melodious whistle.

She ran back down the path and through the gate, and now the rooks were buzzing her. She waved her arms and squinted her eyes almost shut; she touched nothing, and no claws went for her face. The smell of the birds was shocking, like a bundle of wet laundry left rolled up for far too long.

Across the pavement, and she ran into the same car again. Its rusted bumper scratched at her leg through her jeans. She staggered away and went to her knees. With tears welling in her eyes she screamed again, determined to show anger and rage rather than weakness.

More birds closed in, their claws raking through her hair and becoming entangled, wings flapping against her face, and she saw the orange flash of beaks dangerously close to her eyes.

*This is my nightmare!* And with that thought came a vague memory of what would come next. Lucy-Anne stood and closed her hand around a bird's ragged legs. *And now I throw it*, she thought, throwing the creature, *and now the shadow.*

The whistling changed pitch, and a ripple passed through the rooks. Their screeching died out as if they were concentrating on something else now, not just her. As the birds parted slightly before her, she tried to look past their chaotic wings, moving forward through them, keen to see whoever stood beyond.

The shape appeared. As the birds rose away from the square at last, roosting again on rooftops and in tree canopies, she saw the boy standing thirty yards along the street. He was short and slight, dressed in scruffy black clothing. His hair was a wild dark mop, and his stance was one of casual superiority. His smile too, when it came, communicated a level of confident control.

"They like you," the boy called. "Which means I do as well. They're very choosy, my birds."

"*Your* birds?" Lucy-Anne said.

The boy whistled one more time, a short sharp note, and the rooks fell completely silent.

"My birds." He walked towards Lucy-Anne, and she felt herself unable to move. *Not his whistling*, she thought, *that's not what's rooted me here. It's me. It's my nightmare of the birds, and . . .*

. . . and now she wanted to see what came next.

"I dreamed about your birds," she said.

The boy shrugged as he walked.

"You don't seem surprised."

"Why should I?"

She tried to think of a reason, but none came. "I'm looking for my brother," she said instead, and the boy's face grew more stern.

"You'll die," he whispered. "In the streets, in the ruins, you'll die. If the Choppers don't get you, there are other things that will. North of here . . . wild places."

"And you expect me to—"

"I can help you," the boy said.

"What? Help me look for Andrew?"

He nodded. He paused several feet from Lucy-Anne, looking her up and down with a frankness she found unsettling. There was something birdlike about the way his dark eyes shifted, his hands clawed at the air, and his hair almost looked barbed.

"Why would you do that?" she asked.

"My name's Rook," the boy said, "and I've met you in my dreams."

# CHAPTER FOURTEEN
# THE NOMAD

> The six terrorists who attacked London yesterday have been killed in a shoot-out with a military unit in the West End. Communications into and out of London are down. The biological agent used by the terrorists has not yet been identified, but the whole of the London basin is affected, and travel to and from the city is strictly prohibited. Please help the emergency services and the military to contain this disaster by following these simple guidelines: Anyone trying to enter or approach London will be arrested. Any aircraft attempting to overfly London will be shot down. There follows a list of numbers for concerned relatives . . .
>
> —*UK All-Channel Bulletin,*
> *9:00 a.m. GMT onwards, July 29, 2019*

At seventeen, Jack should have taken Sparky aside at the first opportunity to ask him how it was, was she hot, and to give him all the details. But that would have been in normal times, and these times were far from normal. There was a quietness to Sparky the next morning, and while Jenna helped Ruben and Rosemary prepare the best breakfast they could from old tinned foods, Jack sat beside his friend on the sofa.

"Okay, mate?"

"Yeah."

"Hope today's a bit better than yesterday."

"Well . . ." Sparky began, then he smiled. "Yesterday was mixed."

"What's up?"

Sparky sighed. He scratched at his arm where his brother's name was tattooed, then leaned back and looked up at the ceiling. "We've got no control over any of this, you know? We follow Rosemary from one mess to the next. We lose Lucy-Anne, and can't do anything to try and help or find her, and how bloody frustrating is that?"

"We all feel the same. But Rosemary's right, there's no way of even *guessing* where she is." He drummed his fingers on his knee, tapped his foot. He'd dreamed about Lucy-Anne, but today he could not remember his dreams.

"And last night, Jack. My *first time*. Incredible. And . . . I should be telling Steve about it, you know? I should tell him, and he should laugh and be pleased, and it should be a secret from Mum and Dad because that's just the way it is with brothers . . ." He trailed off, blinking slowly.

"You just told me," Jack said.

Sparky looked at him with tears in his eyes. "Thanks."

"You're welcome. Shithead."

"Ha!" Sparky stood and stretched, leaned sideways so that he could see through the hallway and into the kitchen, then turned back to Jack. "Mate," he whispered, "she was *hot*!"

Emily came down a few minutes later, and they all sat around the kitchen table and ate baked beans, hot dog sausages, and tinned peaches. For what it was, Jack enjoyed it immensely.

He tried not to catch Jenna's eyes, embarrassed, but he felt her glancing at him all through breakfast. When he finally stood to tidy up, he took an empty tin from her hand and she held on tight. He looked at her, and realised what a fool he'd been. She looked so anxious and tense, that when he smiled and winked she seemed to deflate.

"Thank you!" she said as she let go of the tin, but Jack knew the real thanks was for something else entirely. Yeah, he'd certainly been a fool. He'd known that Jenna had liked him, just not how much.

"Ruben will be leaving us soon," Rosemary said. "He's not one for sneaking along dangerous streets and scrambling through tunnels."

"I'd only get stuck," he said, tapping his not inconsiderable stomach.

"Are you going home?" Emily asked, and a dark cloud touched Ruben's face.

"Yes, dear," he said. "All the way home."

"Thanks for taking a bullet out of my guts with your bare hands," Jenna said, raising her bottle of water in a toast.

"Any time."

"Bloody hope not!" Sparky said, and they all laughed.

As they left, Rosemary took a quick look around the house, her expression blank. "Doubt we'll use this place again," she said.

"Why not?" asked Emily.

"Too dangerous, dear. I've stayed here three times myself, and Ruben a couple of times. Too much activity attracts attention."

"So it'll just stay shut up?" Jack asked.

"Yes. Once we're out, I'll drop the key down a gutter grating."

Sparky checked that the coast was clear before they trailed out into the street. It was still early, only seven thirty, and the air was cool and clear. Pigeons cooed softly from window sills and rooftops, a scruffy ginger cat strolled without care along the middle of the road, but apart from that all was quiet.

Rosemary pulled the door closed until it clicked. Jack didn't like thinking about the empty house, and how it could be like that forever. They had filled it with life for a night, and even some love, and now it stood alone and abandoned once again, one of many sad monuments to the foolishness of humanity. There were a hundred thousand buildings like this all over London. Houses were built to be lived in, not left empty, home only to the dust of memories.

They walked along the street, and when they came to a gutter Rosemary dropped the key through the grating. Jack heard a faint splash, and the house was lost to them. If anyone ever explored its insides again, they would have to smash down the door or break a window first.

He noticed Sparky and Jenna share a glance and wondered what they were thinking right then.

Ruben said his goodbyes, sparing Rosemary a hug. They seemed very close. Jack and his friends gave their quiet thanks, then the fat man sauntered away, his incredible hands swinging by his sides. *There goes another miracle*, Jack thought. The city killed by humans seemed full of miracles today.

Rosemary huddled them together at the end of the street. She listened for a minute, head cocked, but there was nothing to hear except the birds.

"It's not too far until we go back belowground," she said. "As I told you, Jack, she spends most of her time down in the old Tube station. But I promised to be honest with you from now on, so I have to tell you, the place is disguised. And it's protected from the Choppers."

"Protected how?" he asked, instantly fearing the worst. *Alligators? Lions? Monsters?*

"There are two people down there, boy and girl twins, whose seventh sense has been incredibly boosted."

"Seventh?" Emily asked.

"That's what they call it, for want of a better description. They can project images and ideas onto people's minds. It's remarkable . . . and it can be really quite disturbing, too. Everyone who goes down there has to pass through the twins' projections. Those who should know about the hospital can work through them, because they know the images are false. Anyone else . . . they wouldn't go very far."

"What sort of images?" Jack asked.

Rosemary pursed her lips. "They won't be very nice. But I'll tell you when we're getting closer, and you'll all have to . . ."

"Work through it," Jenna finished for her.

"Yes, dear."

"Piece of cake," Sparky said. Jenna glanced at him and smiled, and Jack felt the growing warmth between the two of them. It made him feel good.

"Maybe Lucy-Anne will be down there," he said. But no one answered, and he realised it was a vain hope.

They set off, walking through the early morning streets and watching the wildlife. It was unsettling, and yet beautiful, how so many animals had made the devastated city their home, as if nature had been patiently awaiting its moment. All the usual birds that Jack would expect to see in a city were there; pigeons, sparrows, starlings, blackbirds, magpies, and the occasional robin. But he also saw a woodpecker, wrens, a kingfisher skimming a canal, goldfinches, siskins, and several pairs of buzzards circling with their offspring. The untempered plant growth throughout the city sustained many more seed-eating birds, and close behind them came the birds of prey.

The birdsong barely lessened as they walked along the street. The creatures were confident. That, Jack thought, was the unsettling part of it. This was no longer a city of people where the birds had to find their own way to survive. Now, the situation had been reversed.

Rosemary made them pause every few minutes and hide in a garden or an alleyway, just to take time to listen and watch for any dangers. They heard no motors, though once an aircraft flew past high overhead. It was fast and loud, and obviously military. Rosemary made them hide in a burnt-out shop, afraid of the detection technology the aircraft might have.

After the aircraft had gone, and as they approached a road junction, a lioness stepped into view from the street perpendicular to theirs. She was sleek and fit-looking, and she paused to look their way.

Jack gasped. Emily, walking beside him, slowly lifted her camera and started to film. The others froze in place.

"Amazing," Sparky whispered.

"Be still and quiet," Rosemary said. Jack saw her take hold of the gun hanging by its strap from her shoulder.

They were close enough to see the lioness's nostrils flare as she sniffed at them. She looked the other way, perhaps deciding whether the street ahead seemed more inviting than the street with the human meat, then stared back at them for a long time.

"Do they eat . . . ?" Jenna was unable to finish, but everyone knew what she meant.

"I've never heard of it," Rosemary muttered. "Too many cats, dogs, and other things for them to hunt."

"Always a first time for everything," Sparky said. Then he giggled. "Jenna tastes good."

"Shut it, or I'll cut you and push you towards her," Jenna whispered.

"Quiet!" Rosemary said. "All of you."

The creature was beautiful. Jack could not help marvelling at how she had adapted to the strange environment, an animal designed to live on the African plains stalking concrete and brick streets and eating dog meat instead of gazelle or zebra. Two years previously she must have been caged in a zoo or wildlife park, meat thrown in to her every day already dead. Now, she had to hunt for every meal. *Nature's way of coping*, he thought. It was wonderful.

Humankind, in its ignorance and superiority, had set itself apart from nature, and that weird chemical or bug released two years before had removed them even further from the evolutionary chain. Ironic that it had been called Evolve.

The lioness roared softly, as if to assure her place in their memories. Then she walked away, disappearing around the building at the corner of the junction.

"That was cool," Sparky said, the excitement apparent in his voice.

"We should move on," Rosemary said. "If she returns with the rest of her pride, things might be different."

They walked for an hour, skirting around a large park that had taken on the appearance of a jungle. The trees at its boundary were full and lush, and where they could see past the trunks there were huge swaths of shrubs with exotic-looking pink flowers drooping from stems a dozen feet tall. They reminded Jack of the blooms they had seen atop the mass grave in Tooting, but these seemed more natural and innocent.

As they approached a roundabout from which four roads branched, Emily paused and pointed.

"Who's that lady?" she said.

They all looked, and for a moment Jack had trouble seeing who she meant. Then he saw the motionless shape on the small concrete island at the roundabout's centre, something he'd taken upon first glance to be a statue, and the breath was knocked from him.

There was something . . . *otherworldly* about the woman. She stood utterly motionless, and between blinks she was suddenly walking towards them, flowing, floating across the dusty tarmac like a ghost. *Her feet* are *touching the ground*, Jack tried to persuade himself. *She* is *walking, not drifting*. She seemed to be moving too quickly.

"Superior?" Jenna asked. None of them could take their eyes

from the woman. Her movement was hypnotic, her face mesmerising.

"Rosemary?" Jack prompted. The woman was coming closer, and a pang of fear complemented his sense of wonder. Her loose jacket flowed behind her, though there was no breeze this morning, and her long hair flicked at the air. "*Rosemary!*"

"The Nomad," Rosemary whispered, and she started backing away.

"Holy shit," Jenna said.

*Nomad*? Jack knew the name, and the legend, but he had always thought it was just that: myth, not truth. A wondrous fable concocted out of the awfulness of what had happened. It spoke of a woman, the Nomad, who wandered the streets of the Toxic City untouched and untouchable. Rumour had it that she possessed all the powers of the Irregulars combined, which made her, so far as those interested in her believed, a god. And that was why Jack could never believe, because the need to have faith in something so amazing after events so dreadful just seemed too obvious.

Out of all of them, it was Jenna who researched and believed in the Nomad the most. Having lost no one to Doomsday, her interest was otherwise.

"Nomad, indeed," a woman's voice said, and it was low and husky as though not used to speech. "No need to flee, healer." She raised one hand and Rosemary stopped backing away, although it looked as if she was still trying.

When the woman reached them at last she continued walking, snaking through and around their small group. Jack thought about moving, but decided against it. None of them moved. Maybe none of them could.

Rosemary was shaking with fear. She had closed her eyes, and she uttered unheard words to herself. Perhaps she was singing a song, or speaking to someone she had lost, anything to take her someplace else.

*Is she so terrible?* Jack thought, looking at the Nomad as she passed before him. She gave him a coy glance, and he felt a warm glow in his chest. He did not recognise it: Fear? Calmness? Lust?

"Are you *really* the Nomad?" Jenna asked.

The woman gave the girl a slow nod as she walked in front of her.

"So are you an Irregular? A Superior? I heard you have many powers, and that—"

"I've no need to name myself other than Nomad."

Emily was filming. She seemed unafraid. *To have her sense of innocence*, Jack thought.

"No one can touch you," Jenna said, and she displayed no fear. Only wonder. "The Choppers can't catch you, the Superiors can't take you. And now I see you, I *recognise* you, and it's all true. You're Angelina Walker. You're the scientist who crashed into the London Eye and spread the infection."

"I'm the first vector, if you need to name a first."

"No need," Jenna said. "I would ask you why, but . . ."

"She's moved on," Jack said. He glanced at Rosemary again, and the woman was still trying to be somewhere else.

Nomad continued to weave around them, and every time she passed before Jack she would give him that strange smile. She seemed to be moving through water.

The air around him felt heavy and thick, and he was not sure he could move even if he wanted to. Nomad performed an occasional, strange dance with her hands, and perhaps she was snatching their breaths from the air. Jack's mind felt open to view, and though there was no sense of being invaded, still he felt exposed and vulnerable to some far greater force.

She passed him again, smiled, moved on.

Emily continued to film. Nomad seemed not to mind, though Jack doubted there would be any recorded image of her when they viewed it back.

The aura she exuded was one of great power. Every one of Jack's senses—normal, unaltered, innocent of the touch of the Toxic City—thrummed with the idea of what Nomad possessed. He saw her movements and her smiles, and her knowledge was so much more. He smelled a sweet, mysterious scent on the air, like perfume from another world. The air tasted of somewhere he'd never been, the sound of her voice was a secret to unfold, and his whole body tingled in her presence, as though touched by colours he had never seen. She was beautiful, wondrous, and terrifying.

"I have a friend," Jack said, "Lucy-Anne. We lost her. Do you know where she is?"

Nomad paused before him and changed direction, passing so close behind him that he felt the hairs on the back of his neck stand up. "She's a wild girl with the birds," Nomad said.

"What does that mean?" Jenna asked.

"Not dead," the strange woman sang. "Just wild."

Jack sighed in relief, and he felt a grey mass of guilt lifting from him. The air seemed to swallow it away.

"Unchanged," Nomad said, "apart from the healer. All of you . . . so pure and untouched."

"I'm Reaper's son," Jack said.

"Reaper? Just another name. Nothing to me, when I walk to spread the word."

"What word?" Jack asked, and he thought, *To some of them, she's a god.*

"The word of change."

"You've changed everything anyway," Jenna said. "You were the one. You were the terrorist."

"Terrorist?" Nomad's flowing walk continued, and she seemed to be tasting the word, considering its meaning. "It *was* all about freedom," she said. "And it's only just begun."

Jack tried to step forward but could not. Rosemary seemed to have entered a trance-like state, still muttering words none of them could hear. "Why is Rosemary so scared of you?" she asked.

"People are scared of what they cannot know."

"I'm not," Sparky said.

Nomad did not answer, and Jack saw Jenna reach out and take Sparky's hand. He did not know whether it took a strength of will, or if Nomad allowed them the contact.

"I think you're the one I want," the woman whispered in Jack's ear. He felt her breath against his neck and a sexual thrill warmed through him. But when she paused before him, halting at last, he knew this was much more than that. Beneath the sexual excitement nestled a fear he had never known before. A fear of the unknown, not without, but within.

"Me?" he said.

"Jack?" Emily said. His sister was scared, but he could not even turn to look at her. This woman, this Nomad, held his complete attention in the palm of her outstretched hand.

"I always knew I'd need help," she said, slipping her index finger into her mouth. Then she reached out, pointing at Jack's mouth. He pressed his lips closed, but still they opened. He leaned back, but stretched forward. He closed his eyes but saw, and he understood that none of this was her. It was all him. Whatever it was she offered, he wanted it completely.

Her finger passed across his tongue and it tasted unknowable. When she withdrew it the taste was gone. But he would know it forever.

"Jack?" Sparky asked.

"It's okay," Jack said, to all of them. "I'm fine."

Nomad gave him that coy smile one more time, and then without another word she walked past them and along the street.

They turned to watch her go. Rosemary slumped down and started shaking, but the others could not take their eyes off the strange woman. She drifted away. Even when she turned out of sight along another road they watched, as if the ghost of her passing would always be here.

"Well, that was weird," Sparky said. He was looking at Jack. "What was all that about?"

"Don't know," Jack said. He moved his tongue about his mouth, and still recalled the taste of that alien touch. He had no idea what she had done, only that she had done something.

"That was Nomad," Jenna said, amazed. "Even after all this time, I was never really sure. But to be here, and to see her . . ." She looked at Jack as well, and he thought he saw a flash of jealousy in her eyes.

"Bugger," Emily said. She was looking at the display screen on the back of her camera, pressing buttons to snap between pictures and bits of film. "It wasn't filming."

"Rosemary's coming to," Jenna said. The woman was looking around, seeing them as if for the first time.

"Is it gone?" she asked.

"Nomad?"

"Is it gone?"

"Yes," Emily said. "She's gone."

"Which way?"

Jack pointed along the street, back the way they had come.

"Then we go that way," Rosemary said. She pointed in the opposite direction.

When they started walking again, Rosemary would not answer

any of their questions. She shook her head when they mentioned Nomad, refused to elaborate on her fear, said nothing when Jenna talked to her about the strange woman. Jack felt angry, but he let his anger filter away, carried on his own thoughts of Nomad.

A few minutes later, still walking in silence, they paused in an old garage forecourt while a group of a dozen people ran by. They were dirty and wild, some of them naked, others dressed in scars. A few growled or whimpered as they ran, and several dribbled blood and mucus from their mouths.

Some loped like animals.

Rosemary did not seem too concerned about hiding.

"The sick ones?" Jack asked. Rosemary did not reply, so he answered for himself. "The ones who can't take it." They all watched the people disappear along the street, and a couple of minutes later Rosemary led them away again.

They walked quickly and as they reached the mouth of Stockwell Tube Station, the healer seemed pleased when they left the sunlight and found cool shadows.

"Down," she said. "We'll be there soon. But once we reach the platform, remember the twins. You'll see things that scare you. But they're not really there." Without another word she pulled a small torch from her pocket and started down the escalators.

Jack and the other followed. Back into the darkness.

And when they stepped onto the platform, Jack saw the first of the giant scorpions.

# CHAPTER FIFTEEN
# HEALERS

There *were* no terrorists. There *is* no help. London is dying, and we're all dying with it.

—*Radio ham communication out of London (first and last transmission), 11:44 a.m. GMT, July 29, 2019*

He could see why the unwary would choose to go no further.

The scorpions were as fat as Jack's head, their legs as long as his arms, and there were too many to count. Some were bright yellow, stings dripping tears of poison that sizzled small holes in the floor tiles. Others were black, with red markings on their backs and spikes along their legs on which rotten meat festered. They hissed and spat at each other, crawled up the shattered tile walls, balanced along the dulled rails where trains used to run, dropped from the ceiling, and a group of them further along the platform worried at a pile of fresh bodies, ripping flesh, and breaking bones.

*They're not real*, Jack thought. Rosemary walked into a scorpion and it disappeared around her feet, melting away into a breath of mist and shadow. *Living in my mind, that's all. They're not here. They're not real*. He closed his eyes and opened them again, and the scorpions were multiplying and growing larger.

"I can't!" Emily said. "The snakes. The *snakes*!"

"I see scorpions," Jack said. He held his sister's hand, and the sweat on her palm added to his own.

"Chickens," Sparky said.

"Chickens?" Jack laughed nervously.

"Ten feet tall," the boy said defensively. "Beaks are covered in blood, and—"

"You are truly weird."

"They're not here," Rosemary said, her voice cool and flat. "None of this is here."

"What do you see?" Jack asked, but the woman did not respond. Since their meeting with the Nomad she had been distant, and he vowed to ask her why. But right now, his mind was focussed on his mother. She was down here in the dark, his dear, lovely mum, and soon they would be together again.

Emily looked at him and smiled. "Not real snakes," she said.

"Not real scorpions," Jack said.

"I see moths as big as seagulls," Jenna said.

"My chickens will take your moths any day," Sparky said, and they all laughed. The edgy banter continued as they made their way along the platform, helping each other walk past and through their own unique fears. Jack's attention turned inward, and he tried to sense whether the twins Rosemary had mentioned were touching him inside to plant these fears, or causing him to project them himself. If he closed his eyes he could still hear the scorpions, though he had yet to feel their cool, sharp touch. He could understand how the twins were such an effective defence: what he saw was terrifying, even though he understood it was not real. To anyone unsuspecting, seeing a Tube platform crawling, squirming, or sliming with their own personal fears would be unbearable.

They walked to the end of the platform, and Rosemary shone her torch into the tunnel. There was a ledge leading in there, just wide enough to shuffle along sideways, and the others followed her as she started edging her way inside.

Something squealed, and Jenna let out a sharp scream.

"The rats are real," Rosemary said.

"Thanks."

The wall at their backs ended suddenly, and by the time they were all through Rosemary was a dozen feet ahead of them, talking quietly to someone sitting in an armchair. The furniture was so incongruous that Jack wondered if he was still seeing things. But the girl was still in the chair, a boy sitting beside her on a camp bed, and he knew they were almost there.

"The twins," Jenna whispered. "What power! It's scary, isn't it?"

"It's wonderful," Emily said.

*It's both*, Jack thought. *Just like everything these London survivors can do, it's both.*

Rosemary waved them all over and shone her torch at a metal door in the wall behind the twins. "In there," she said. "Down a spiral staircase to an old deep level shelter. They built it during the Second World War, and now it's found its use again." She smiled at Jack and Emily.

"Does she know we're coming?" Emily asked.

"No. I never told her I was going for you. It was a secret, and . . . I didn't want to raise her hopes. It'll be a nice surprise."

*A nice surprise.* It was the phrase Jack and his friends used for something amazing. He was certain it was going to be just that.

He and Emily went alone, the others remaining up on the platform to give them their moment. He glanced at Sparky as the metal door closed behind them, feeling awkward and embarrassed, but his friend beamed a smile and gave him a big thumbs-up.

Beyond the door was a small metal landing, then a staircase that spiralled down into the darkness. Its walls moved, flexing in the flickering light from candles placed on every third or fourth riser. Jack went first, and the candlelight moved even more.

He heard Emily descending behind him.

He was nervous, and scared, and his heart beat so fast that his vision seemed to throb. *We're going to see Mum*, he thought. In his memory she was always alive, but in his mind's eye he sometimes found her dead. This descent felt so surreal and unbelievable. He paused on the spiral staircase and breathed in deeply, and Emily did not ask why he had stopped. He heard her taking in a big breath as well.

The staircase ended, and Jack ducked through a narrow doorway. They were at the end of a very long room, twice the length of the platform up above. It had a similar vaulted brick ceiling and tiled walls. A generator hummed somewhere, and strings of light bulbs were suspended from the ceiling. There were three lines of beds, maybe fifteen in each line, and at the far end of the room, two curtained areas. Along one wall stood metal storage cabinets, desks and shelving, and two doors leading away into other rooms beyond.

About half of the beds were taken. Several people wandered from bed to bed, giving drinks, touching patients, and Jack spotted his mother immediately.

"There," he said, grabbing Emily's arm and pointing.

"I see her," his sister said, and her voice broke.

They watched their mother for a minute, remembering the way she moved, brushed her hair back from her forehead, and laughed, and then it was too much and Emily dashed forward, unable to call out through her tears.

The sobbing was enough. Jack saw their mother stiffen, her back to them, and her stillness told him that she already knew.

"Mum," he said.

It was stranger than he'd ever thought it could be, because his mother had changed so much. She was thinner than before, her hair shorter, an ugly scar beside her nose, and though he knew it was impossible, her fingers seemed longer and more delicate. She had aged ten years in the two since they had parted.

But she was still their mother, and as she hugged them both and Jack smelled her familiar smells, he realised that this reunion must be even stranger for her. Emily had been seven when they'd come to London, now she was nine. The change in her was greater than all of them, and that showed in their mother's eyes as she kept pulling back and staring at her daughter.

They went into one of the side rooms, which was stacked all around with towels, beddings, and bags of medical supplies. There was a space in the middle with a large table and several chairs, mugs, and plates scattered across its surface. More tears and hugs were inevitable, but eventually the talking had to start. There were two years and a whole new world to catch up on.

So Jack told his mother how he had been looking after Emily, living in the house they'd shared ever since he was born, and how Emily had helped him as much as he had helped her. He said he'd always tried to keep the faith that she and his father were still alive somewhere in the Toxic City. He told her about the doubts he and others had about the government's lies, but that the general populace believed that London was now a city of deadly, toxic monsters. He had met his best friends—Sparky, Jenna, and Lucy-Anne—through the growing certainty that they were all being lied to.

His mother said how proud she was of her brave children, and how not a day had gone by since Doomsday when she had not thought about them and felt desperate for them to be together again.

Whenever Jack mentioned their father, she changed the subject. For now, he allowed her that.

He and Emily took turns relating their journey into London, and when he mentioned Rosemary, his mother smiled and shook her head. "She's become a good friend. As good as any friend can be in this place, at least."

"She came to get us because of Reaper," Jack said.

She stared at him for a while, then turned to Emily, speaking past her constant veil of tears. "How are you doing in school, my darling?"

Their mother told them how unbearable it was being separated from her children. Soon after Doomsday, when London stank with the dead and resounded with the agonised cries of those unfortunates still alive, many had attempted to make their way back to family and home. The slaughter had been terrible. She'd seen five people pulled from a car and executed outside a church in Holborn, the military still wearing their bulky NBC suits, still uncertain about what had happened. Every survivor could relate tales of killings from that time. Since then there had been fewer and fewer efforts to escape.

"It became like another world," she said. "I convinced myself that London was a different place entirely, a different reality, not just the ruin of a city so close to home. I missed you both terribly, but thinking that way made it somehow easier."

"It's not so wrong," Jack said. "We've only been here for two days, but it *is* somewhere else."

Their mother told them about the hospital, and how difficult it was gathering medicines, bedding, towels, and food without being caught by the Choppers, the problems of sanitation, wild animals, rats . . .

Emily asked why they needed medicines when there were healers. Their mother replied that most healers' powers were very specific, and that illnesses and injuries in the Toxic City were much more diverse.

They were talking around so many important subjects, and the more they talked, the more Jack began to fear they would never discuss what was important.

"Rosemary says you're a healer like her," he said. And here it was. The subject of their mother's change, that in turn would lead on to what had happened to their father.

"Not like her," she said. "Not exactly. None of them . . . none of *us* . . . are *exactly* alike."

"What was it like, Mum? When it happened?"

She shook her head slowly, her face grim. She looked between Jack and Emily and into the past, seeing scenes which Jack guessed she had tried her best to bury. But her daughter had asked, and the good mother would answer.

"It was like living a nightmare. First the rumours of explosions and a terrorist attack, and then . . . Your father and I were just coming out of the Natural History Museum. There wasn't panic, but police cars were tearing along the roads in every direction, sirens everywhere, and people . . ." She shook her head, smiling. "People were standing with their phone cameras, ready to catch something amazing. A few were watching the news on their phones, and as we stood on the pavement we could almost see the ripples of panic spreading out from these people. That was the first time we heard talk of a biological attack, and your father and I started to worry.

"The first people I saw die were coming out of a restaurant on a street corner. Maybe the breeze blew whatever was in the air along the street, and it hit them just as they emerged. They fell, hard and quick. I knew they hadn't just fainted. You could almost see the life going from them."

"They died that quickly?"

"Everyone did. The breeze carried the change through the streets, and one breath was enough. They fell in waves, and the sound was . . . horrible. Heads striking pavements. Mothers dropping their dead babies, falling dead themselves. Cars crashed. There were explosions, fires. There was screaming."

"But you and Dad?"

"We ran. We thought we were running away from it, but then they started dying all around us. And then we fell." She was crying now, but these tears were far different from those she had already shed. They glimmered on a sad face, not a happy one, and they did not seem quite so bright. "We lay together on the pavement, side by side, looking into each other's faces. I saw his eyes go red as the veins in them gave out, and I felt a stab of pain in my own head, and I thought, *That's it*. The last thing I thought about was . . . was you. I think I spoke to you both, as I lay there. I closed my eyes, waiting . . . And when I opened them again it was night, and your father was gone."

Jack had a million more questions, but he could see that his mother was finding this difficult.

"I never saw him again." She shook her head, smiled at Jack, and hugged her daughter for the hundredth time.

"And when you woke up, you were changed?" he asked. Meeting Rosemary and the others, seeing what they could do, had been incredible. But sitting here now and realising that his mother was one of them shocked him to the core.

"Not that I noticed right away. It took a while for whatever happened to us all to really come to the fore. That day I spent wandering the streets, trying to find help, trying to find somewhere not clogged with bodies. I called for Graham, kept calling. My phone didn't work, so I tried some of those I found dropped in the street. They were all dead, too. The electricity was already off. It's never been back on since. Later that day, the sounds of shooting began. I hid in a hotel, and I was there for several days. There was bombing, most of it far away, some quite near. I saw planes flying high overhead. I don't know what they were targeting, and for a while I was afraid they were going to just bomb the whole city.

"Some of the blasts blew glass from the window, and I got this." She touched the scar beside her nose. "It hurt terribly, but as I touched it in front of the mirror . . . I *knew* I could do something about it. And it was as if knowing I could do something helped, because the cut started to heal. It took ten minutes. I wasn't surprised or upset, shocked or scared. It felt natural, and if anything, I was a little annoyed that I couldn't heal it any better. But that was right at the beginning, and my ability has improved with time.

"I waited, expecting help. But when I saw people moved through the streets, I was suddenly too scared to call to them. And it was Rosemary who found me."

Emily seemed content to cuddle into her mother and hear the sound of her voice. She even seemed sleepy. But Jack was filled with more questions, *many* more, so many that he wondered whether they would ever be able to talk normally with each other again.

There was one question screaming to be asked.

"Dad. Reaper. Please tell me."

She looked at him for a long time, studying his face. "I didn't know he was still alive until six months ago."

"He didn't try to find you?"

She shook her head. "He's not Graham anymore, Jack."

"Not my daddy?" Emily asked.

"No, baby. He's changed much more than anyone else I know, or have heard about. I saw Reaper once, from a distance, and though I recognised him, I also knew he was someone else. And everything they say about him . . ." She frowned and looked away.

"You're still wearing the locket he bought you," Jack said.

His mother smiled sadly and fingered the jewellery. "Of course. My husband gave me this, and I loved him very much."

"Rosemary left London to get me so that I could speak to Dad. Persuade him to join his Superiors with everyone else and fight their way out of London."

His mother seemed genuinely shocked, and she sat back and

stared up at the ceiling for a while. "Everyone's so desperate," she said. "It's tragic. There's so much good in what's left of this place, but no hope at all."

"I'll speak to him. I've already said I would, but I insisted on coming to you first."

"I've no hope left for him, Jack. I've heard about the things he's done. He's very, very dangerous now. You understand? He's . . ." she trailed off again.

"He's killed people."

"I cure, he kills." She was going to ask him not to go, he knew that. The request would come soon. But the more his mother betrayed loss of hope for his father, the more determined Jack was becoming to talk to him.

"He won't hurt me," Jack said.

"Your father died when I was lying beside him on that pavement. The man you might find, Reaper, is someone else. Please, son, don't—"

"Mum." He noticed that Emily was asleep now, and he moved closer so that he could hug them both together. "I've got to try. You see that? I've spent two years trying to find my way here. I can't just abandon him now."

"The Choppers, the soldiers, there's just no way out for any of us."

"It's not for anyone else I'll be doing it," he said. "It's for us: you, Emily, me. We need him. *I* need him. I need my dad."

"He's not your dad anymore," she said quietly. Then she sighed, put her arm around him, and hugged him back. The three of them sat there for a while, saying no more, content just to be with each other. Jack was overjoyed. But the joy was shadowed by the knowledge of what he had to do next and the terrible fear that he might fail.

Sparky and Jenna came down, and Jack introduced his mother to them as Susan. He told her they were his best friends.

Rosemary was with them, and when the women spoke it was with a reserve that perhaps had not been there before. That was not Jack's fault. And truly, he did not care. Rosemary had helped them and healed them when it was needed, but she had also led them willingly into danger and between the literal jaws of death. And the more he thought about how things had worked out so far, the more he believed she had used them all.

Jack took a moment to look around the hospital. After a few minutes, his mother finished talking with Rosemary and came to join him. Hidden away in the curtained area were several terribly sick people, and his mother said she had no idea what ailed them. Her gift was healing, but only physical alterations responded to her particular touch—wounds, cuts, and broken bones. Rosemary was slightly different in that she could also sense a sickness inside and, if it was something out of place, or something that should not be there, heal it. She had taken cancers from people, fixed faulty heart valves. But neither woman could combat the invisibly small invaders of infection.

"So aren't these all Irregulars?" he asked.

"Yes. Everyone in London now is an Irregular, apart from the Choppers and those in their employ. But they came in after Doomsday. Those of us who survived the Evolve virus . . . yes, all changed."

"So what do they do?"

His mother pointed at an old man on a bed close to them. "Richard was a Pleader. In the right conditions, he could exert his will and desires on the chaos around us, and coax it in a certain direction."

"Change the future?"

"In small leaps, and on a very small scale. But no more. Whatever he has is killing him." She sounded very sad. "Over there, that big lady, she had hearing better than a dog's. Massive audio range. She's deaf, now."

"Is it the same illness that Richard has?"

"It looks the same, but I just don't know. I'm no doctor, and it was Doomsday that made me a healer."

"We saw people out on the streets, naked and raving. Like animals."

"The same," his mother said. "We're seeing it more and more."

"The Irregulars are starting to die," Jack whispered, and his mother said nothing to contradict.

Emily ran up to them from where Jenna and Sparky were standing. Jack looked at Richard and the other dying people, treasuring their reunion even more.

"We met the Nomad," he mentioned, thinking of how she had picked on him and the taste of her finger in his mouth. He felt his mother tense.

"You really saw her?" she said, aghast.

"She said that was her name. And she was . . . strange."

Susan shook her head. "Most people don't really believe in her, even now."

"Jenna does. She's collected all the stories. She think she's Angelina Walker, the woman who crashed into the Eye and released Evolve."

"The first vector."

"That's what she called herself, yeah."

"What did she do? What did she say?"

Jack was not sure why he lied. But when he said, "Nothing, really," and glancing down at Emily, his sister gave him a little smile. He knew then that he'd made the correct decision.

"Strange," his mother said.

"Huh!" Jack said. "Strange? Did I tell you about the lioness? And the wolves we heard, and the flowers in Tooting?"

She smiled and shook her head. "No, but I'm sure you're going to."

"I want Emily to tell you, Mum. I want her to show you." He held Emily's hand. They'd already talked about this, and now the physical contact gave him double the strength he needed. "I want you and Emily to get out, the way we got in. Rosemary's already said she'll take you. She has a gun, and knows where she can get more."

"Guns, Jack?" She used her old scolding voice, and Jack almost smiled. Almost.

"For the dogs, Mum. And . . . anything else that might try to stop you."

"And you?" Her voice quavered. *She's afraid of losing me again*, he thought. And he understood. The temptation to leave was there, but he had to preserve faith in their father, a faith he could never lose without at least trying.

"I've already told you what I'll be doing, Mum."

"I like that word," she said. "'Mum.' It's a good word."

"I always knew I'd get to use it again."

"And Dad," Emily said. "That's another good word. Jack says it has power."

His mother's eyes opened wider, and he saw something that might have been hope. Or if not that, then acceptance of his need to try. She came to him and rested her head on his shoulder.

"Be very, very careful," she said. *Pleaded.*

"I will, Mum. Sparky and Jenna are coming with me."

"Are they special forces?"

He laughed. "Not quite. But we're a good team."

She nodded, squeezed his hand, and then parted. "I have to speak to my friends down here, tell them . . . something. Not the truth. I couldn't do that to them."

"Will leaving . . . ?"

"Compared to everything else we've been through?" She looked around, smiling at a patient walking with the aid of a wheeled frame. "It'll be sad, rather than hard."

"Sis, you look after Mum, won't you?"

"You betcha!" Emily stood slightly in front of their mother, like a bodyguard preparing to take a bullet. Her face was so stern that Jack laughed out loud.

The thought of leaving his mother so soon after finding her again was incredibly painful. But the longer they remained together, the less inclined he'd be to leave at all. And he owed his father everything.

"That camera," he said to Emily. "It's precious. It's almost priceless, for all the people we've seen in London. You know that, don't you?"

"Of course I do! I'm not a bloody kid, you know."

"I know you're not, Emily. You're my hero."

"See, Mum?" she said, beaming proudly. "Jack's hero!"

"So when you get out, put the camera somewhere safe and sound. Don't take it home with you. When I come out with Sparky and Jenna, we'll retrieve it and do what we can."

"And Dad?" Emily said.

"I'll do my best."

"Why does he call himself Reaper now?" his little sister asked.

"Because he's forgotten who he is. I'm going to remind him."

"Please keep them safe," Jack said to Rosemary.

The old woman smiled. "Keep *yourself* safe. Good luck with Reaper."

"His name's Graham. And I'm looking forward to seeing my father again." Jack knew what she *wanted* to hear: *I'll speak to him, persuade him, plead with him if I have to*. But he could not say that yet, because his priority was completing his family. Perhaps the two aims would run side by side, or maybe they would collide. Time would tell.

Jack, Sparky, and Jenna watched them leave the underground hospital. Jenna put an arm around Jack's shoulder.

"Wimp," Sparky muttered, and Jack coughed, half-laugh, half-sob.

Jack saw his mother and sister pass out of sight, and he could not fight away the feeling that he would never see his family again. Standing there with his two best friends in the world, he had never felt so alone.

# CHAPTER SIXTEEN
# ON REAPER'S SHOULDERS

Birmingham is the new capital city of Great Britain.

*—Government Proclamation, 3:44 p.m. GMT, July 29, 2019*

Lucy-Anne was too terrified to ask him about his dreams. Her own scared her enough. So she walked with Rook in silence, and he told her they had somewhere special to go.

"But I need to find Andrew," she said.

"And you've told me where he is. 'North of here,' you said."

"Yeah."

"Girl . . . *where* north of here?" She still hadn't told him her name, because in some ways it still felt distant to her. It belonged to a girl with other friends, another life.

"Well . . ." she began, but there was little else she could say. *Your brother is alive north of here*, she remembered a man saying, and if that was all he'd said, perhaps that thing in her mind would not have snapped. But he had gone on, told her more.

"North is a big place," Rook said. "And like I mentioned, it's a *wild* place." He looked up at the clear blue sky, speckled with hundreds of dark spots where the rooks kept pace with them. "Everywhere in the city is wild now."

"So where are you taking me?" she asked.

Rook laughed, and high above Lucy-Anne heard the cawing of many birds.

"Girl, I don't believe I can take you anywhere. But if you'll come with me, I'll introduce you to some people who might help."

"Why might they?"

He frowned a little, looked away, but then smiled at her again. "Because I'll ask them."

The boy seemed friendly enough to Lucy-Anne. And he was strong, not just in his wiry frame, but mentally. He exuded a power that frightened her a little, but alongside that fright she had to admit it turned her on as well. His was a power she had never imagined, and something about the fact he had changed his name made him seem closer to the city. She had come to this place with friends, but they paled when compared to Rook.

"Okay," she said. "But first I have to pee."

Rook glanced around, then pointed at an overgrown parking lot beside a burnt-out pub. "Public toilets!" he said, giggling at his own joke.

Lucy-Anne dashed across the road, feeling his eyes burning into her back. His dark eyes. *So like a rook's*, she thought, *almost lifeless*. But the rest of his face made up for it; he always wore a smile, and there were laughter lines in his young man's skin.

He was dangerous, but for now she felt safe around him.

For now.

Rosemary had told them which way to go. No one really knew where Reaper could be found, but there were rumours. *North, across the river, into the heart of the city, and look out for the rooks. One of the boys that runs with Reaper communes with them. Last I heard, they were seen above St. James's Park.*

As they crossed Vauxhall Bridge, Jack remembered a dozen movies that had used this place as a setting. He'd often heard his father describing London as a giant film set, and now here he was, in a depressing movie about a sad future. Two years ago, who could have believed that London would ever look like this?

The Houses of Parliament, once home to the British Government, was a ruin. One half of it looked as though it had suffered sustained bombing, and there was little recognisable left. The other half had burned, and though most of its walls were still standing, they were swathed in a thick green climbing plant erupting with violet flowers. The once-smart lawns outside, where Jack had watched countless politicians being interviewed for TV and Net-News, was a plain of waist-high grass and graceful bamboo.

The Big Ben tower was still there, but the clock faces had been blown out, and Jack could see straight through its upper section. The bell itself seemed to have gone. Perhaps they would find it, if they looked long enough, fallen and covered in moss. But that would gain them nothing. Time flicked at him with its cruel whip, though as yet Jack was unsure why he felt such urgency.

Perhaps it was those dying Irregulars in the underground hospital.

They paused on the bridge for a while, catching their breath, taking a drink and looking down the River Thames. It flowed through a wild place now. Clumps of detritus—plants, branches, broken things—drifted down from upriver, gently bobbing towards the sea. A couple of the old river cruisers were still there, one of them wedged beneath one of the gentle arches of Grosvenor Bridge, the other still moored at river's edge not far from where they stood. From this distance it looked strangely peaceful and serene, so much so that it seemed out of place. A picture postcard image of hell.

"I'm glad you two got together," Jack said. They had not talked much since leaving the Underground again, though the silence was never uncomfortable.

"Me too," Sparky said grinning at Jenna.

"I don't know what came over me," she said. "I thought I'd been shot in the gut, not the head."

They all laughed softly, and watched an eagle drift majestically along the river's course and pass beneath the bridge.

"Wow," Jack whispered. "Wonder where the hell *that* came from."

"You know, Jack," Jenna said, "Lucy-Anne will . . . we'll find her and . . ."

He shook his head. "Knowing she's alive is good."

"You believe Nomad?"

"Don't you?"

"Without a doubt." Jenna still seemed awkward, and Jack wasn't sure he wanted to verbalise his thoughts. But really, this was no time for any sort of self-deception.

"Me and Lucy-Anne . . . I think we were finished before we even started. Thrown together by our backgrounds and histories, not because we fancied each other."

"Good friends," Sparky said. "Maybe that's what you two are."

"Yeah," Jack nodded. "What you two did last night . . . Well, we haven't done that for ages."

Jenna blushed and elbowed Sparky in the ribs.

"I said nothing!" he protested. But she was smiling, and Jack laughed.

"Let's get on," he said.

"Rooks," Sparky muttered. "Always spooked the crap out of me."

"Scarier than chickens?" Jenna quipped.

"Okay, okay, another point to Jenna."

They crossed the bridge and passed through Parliament Square, keeping their ears and eyes open.

Walking progressively northward, Jack wondered whether Lucy-Anne had already come this way. He thought of their time together and tried to come to terms with what it had all meant.

They'd gone through the usual boyfriend and girlfriend moments; kissing and cuddling in front of a movie, drinking cider when Emily was in bed, progressing on to awkward fumblings and gasped moments of shared pleasure. But the physical side had always felt somehow false and forced, and it was the times when he talked Lucy-Anne through her fury, doubt, and despair that seemed most important to Jack now. Doomsday had left her with nothing and no-one, and more than anything, he had been there to help her through that. And it had been a natural process. He did not feel even a tiny bit used, and he was certain that Lucy-Anne had welcomed every moment of their unusual relationship. She was a beautiful girl, but his fondest memories of her were when she smiled an honest and happy smile, rather than when she lay half-naked on his sofa.

If only he'd realised that she'd been so close to snapping.

*I'm so bloody grown-up*, he thought without much humour. He looked at Sparky and Jenna, saw their shared smiles and the way they sought physical contact, and his envy was a very gentle thing.

Morning passed into afternoon, and in a side street they found a grocers that didn't smell too bad. The central aisle display of fresh fruit and vegetables was now home to shrivelled black things, like something excavated rather than grown. But there were shelves of tinned foods that had not been touched, and though the labels were faded after two years of dampness, they found some tinned fruit still fit to eat. It tasted sweet, and good.

"Shit," Sparky said.

"What?" Jack was immediately alert, but his friend was still sitting down.

"The door."

Jack looked, and at first he saw nothing. Then he made out the faint, curled gleam of a thin wire, nestled by the door jamb. They must have tripped it on the way in.

Sparky was already looking around the shop. "There," he said. "Old security camera."

"Everything in this place is covered in dust apart from that camera's lens."

"Reaper?" Jenna said.

Jack stood and browsed the shelves, trying to appear calm. "Doubt it," he said. "He's leader of the bloody Superiors. Bet he's got people who can do a lot more than a trip-wire and a camera."

"We should go," Sparky said. "Quickly." As they fled the shop, Jack saw Sparky giving the camera the finger.

They ran along the street, disturbing a pack of dogs that were worrying something newly-dead just inside a house's front door. Luckily most of the dogs ran into the house, not out at them, and Jack kicked out at the one mutt that came too close. Its jaws snapped on thin air, but it did not follow.

They tried to lose themselves, hoping that they would shake off any potential pursuers. But then they heard the sounds of motors in the distance, and they paused at a street corner, panting.

"We *can't* be caught!" Jack said.

"We have to hide." Jenna was pointing at doors both open and closed.

"They might have the whole area wired."

"Well, we can't just stand here arsing about!" Sparky said. "Come on!"

They ran along another street, climbing over a huge wreck where a lorry and several cars had crashed and burned. Jack was aware of a charred skull staring at him through one smashed windscreen, but then something flashed overhead that distracted his attention. A helicopter, its sudden appearance explosive in the street, engine sound dwindling rapidly as it headed away . . . and then started to turn.

"Chopper chopper!" Sparky shouted, giggling nervously.

"We *can't* be caught!" Jack said again. "This isn't fair!" He thought of his mother and sister crawling out of London through the dangerous darkness, his father somewhere to the north, and Lucy-Anne wandering the street alone as she searched the ruin of one of the world's largest cities for her lost brother. And such a weight of responsibility pressed down on him that for a moment he could not move, crushed there on that burnt car's bonnet and staring into the skeletal eyes of someone sorely missed.

"Come on," Sparky said, tapping his leg.

"Jack!" Jenna shouted.

Another helicopter appeared above the end of the street, lowering itself slowly between house rows, rotors so close that they whipped dust from the buildings' facades.

"There!" Jenna shouted, pointing at an open door across the street. "We can go through and try to find—"

"Look!" Sparky shouted. He pointed, but there was no need. The darkening of the sky was obvious.

The helicopter pilot was concentrating so hard on not crashing into the houses that he can't have noticed the flock of rooks gathering above him. There were hundreds of them, perhaps thousands, swirling and waving in complex patterns that were as beautiful as they were disturbing.

"Over there!" Jenna said. Along the street, halfway between where they stood and where the pilot was readying to land, someone emerged from a house. Rooks roosted on his shoulders and head, and though it could not be heard, Jack saw that he was whistling.

The helicopter was ten feet above the ground when the rooks dived into its spinning rotors.

"Down!" Sparky shouted. He pulled Jenna down beside him, Jack fell beside the burnt out cars . . . but they all had to watch.

Thousands of birds exploded in puffs of black and sprays of blood. The houses beside the aircraft were coated in clumps of wet feather and meat, and the combined calls of dying birds was louder that the protesting engine. Some dived into the main rotors, other curved down and flew into the rear rotor blade, their suicides instant and without hesitation.

The helicopter's front windshield was quickly obscured by a mess of diced rooks, and it tipped down and to the left.

Sparky shouted something else, but the noise was too great, the chaos too confusing to hear. The aircraft tilted and hit the ground hard, and the still-spinning rotors smashed across the front of a house. Shards of shattered brick zinged along the street like shrapnel from an explosion, ricocheting from the ruined cars, smashing windows, and whistling overhead. Jack felt something hit his leg, and the impact point quickly turned wet and numb.

The motor squealed, crunched, and then exploded with a pained grinding of metal. A section of brickwork fell from the front of the house directly into the blades, and one of them snapped away, spinning skyward and disappearing over the terraced rooftops. An avalanche of roof slates slid down onto crashed helicopter.

The remaining rotors stopped spinning, broken and dipped, and the aircraft settled at a slant against the house's wall.

Jack could not move. He looked from the ruin of the helicopter, to the boy with rooks on his shoulder, then back to the aircraft. There was movement there, though it could have been the shuffle of dying birds twitching wings or tail feathers. More slates slipped from the roof. An upstairs window fell forward and smashed across a broken rotor blade. The house was still shifting, and the rest of it could come down at any moment.

There were still hundreds of rooks circling above, and the mysterious boy watched them.

A side door on the helicopter creaked open. Two soldiers fell out, stumbling away from the wreck and quickly bringing their weapons to bear.

Behind the boy standing in the house's doorway, Jack saw a shadow move. As it emerged into the light, he could see her face.

"Lucy-Anne!" Sparky shouted. She withdrew at the sound of her name, but they had all seen her. Jenna glanced back at Jack, shocked and afraid, just as Sparky stood and started running diagonally across the road.

One of the soldiers raised his gun and fired.

Jack blinked against the shot, and in the space of that brief darkness he dreaded what he would see when he looked again.

Sparky was still running, hunched down now, and Lucy-Anne had appeared once more, eyes wide with shock, waving him towards her and shouting for him to *Run! Run!*

*He won't miss a second time*, Jack thought, looking along the street at the soldier. The Chopper was changing his stance, settling into a proper shooting posture this time, and behind him the other soldier was taking aim as well.

"Run, Sparky!" Jenna shouted, and the second soldier looked their way.

The circling rooks dived, silent and fast. They moved like a single slice of night, and somewhere in their cries as they powered into the two soldiers, Jack was sure he heard gunshots. The men disappeared, replaced by a vicious cloud of pecking, clawing birds.

More people tumbled from the helicopter. Two soldiers fired into the birds, oblivious to whether they were hitting their companions, and the third man retreated behind the wreck, talking into something in his hand. Jack recognised him: grey hair, short . . . Miller.

As Sparky reached the house and Lucy-Anne greeted him with a confused smile, two doors on that side of the street but closer to the helicopter crashed open. The several people that emerged must have been rushing through the gardens and houses to get here, and Jack guessed they were sorry they had missed all the action. They certainly looked like fighters. One was short and dressed in black, and Jack had difficulty focussing on him . . . almost like a shadow where the sun still shone. Another carried a variety of guns and knives, her eyes milky white and blind. They darted across the street and approached the downed helicopter, working well together, their movements fluid and rehearsed.

Jenna had run after Sparky, and as Jack climbed across the last of the burnt cars, he looked that way, too . . .

. . . and saw his father emerging from an open doorway close to the helicopter.

"Dad," he croaked, his voice hoarse.

His father looked so different. Still tall and trim, but his face carried so much more than his forty-five years now, and his mouth was cruel, laughter lines turned into creases of worry and stress.

"Dad!" Jack shouted at last.

Reaper turned and looked directly at him. For that moment, they were the only two people in the street. Nothing else mattered. Here was his father, missing for two years and considered a lost cause by his wife. Jack tried to welcome a rush of memories similar to when he and Emily had found his mother, but the memories he found were more elusive, and less joyful. They were tinged by the present, and the blank mask that this man had become.

Not even a smile.

"Dad, it's me, Jack!"

Reaper took one step towards his son, then stopped. He turned and said something to the blind Superior now standing by his side, and Jack was terrified that the order had been given to kill him. But the Superior merely walked towards the downed helicopter. Miller was at the ruined aircraft, screaming into the thing in his hand. Two soldiers flanked him, guns at the ready, and rooks were settling all across the wreckage. More circled above, and yet more pecked at red things scattered across the street. Dead birds, dead people; meat was meat.

The second helicopter returned.

"Over here!" Sparky called. He and Jenna were with Lucy-Anne now, and they retreated into the house's shadow.

Jack wanted to run. But even when the helicopter's machine guns opened up, tearing chunks of masonry from the terrace's façade, smashing holes in roofs, shattering those few whole windows that remained, all he could do was look at his father.

The helicopter was hovering above the opposite row of houses, and Reaper faced up to it as bullets impacted all around him. He seemed to be drawing a long, deep breath.

Jack dropped to his stomach just as his father screamed. It was a short, sharp sound, but louder than anything Jack had ever heard before in his life. A grunt of unimaginable volume, it caused a storm of movement across the street: dust and shrapnel was driven away as though by a huge storm; bodies of dead rooks fluttered through the air once more; windows and doors, all but untouched on that side of the street, blew inwards.

The shout struck the helicopter, and it went into a spin. Bullets raked along the street as its guns continued firing, tearing up the ground a few feet from Jack's face and ripping through the tangle of crashed, blackened cars. Then the shooting stopped, and the aircraft dropped as though punched from above. It hit the row of houses and sank in, rotors shredding two roofs of tiles and timber and filling the air with chaos once more. Walls blew out, floors collapsed, and the sudden quiet after the crash was stunning.

Jack lifted himself and looked around to make sure everyone he loved was okay. Sparky and the others peered out from the house once again, and along the street the other Superiors picked themselves up, dusted themselves down.

Reaper stood where he had been before, staring at the downed aircraft. He smiled.

Jack looked at the new wreck as well, and through the ruin of a house's façade he saw movement as people tried to climb from the twisted metal and piled masonry.

The second shout came without warning. More directed this time, still the volume was agonising and unbelievable, and Jack fell to his knees with his hands clasping bloodied ears.

The helicopter exploded. It was a small blast, but the fuel tanks ignited, and the fire spread quickly.

People started screaming.

Reaper was smiling wider now.

"Dad, get them out," Jack said.

"Never call me that," Reaper said. Jack realised that he was more than aware of what was happening, who had found him, and why Jack was here.

It simply did not matter.

The screaming from the burning helicopter was terrible, and Jack walked back and forth with his hands over his ears, hating what he was hearing but unable to do anything about it. He felt the heat of the flames on his back as he turned to his father, and past him to the house. Jenna and Sparky were standing by the front door, holding each other as they watched, but Lucy-Anne was trotting along the street with the boy with rooks on his shoulders.

There were a series of smaller blasts from the fire as ammunition ignited, and the last of the screams was cut off.

"No," Jack said, not wanting to see his dad like this, not wishing to believe the man who had loved him and read to him and played football with him could be standing here with the burnt-flesh smell of his victims hanging in the air. And *smiling*. He was still *smiling*.

Jack ran past his father towards Sparky and Jenna, and as he passed he muttered, "Bastard."

"You okay?" Sparky asked.

"Yeah. You?" Jack's friends nodded.

"You're bleeding," Jenna said, nodding down at Jack's leg. There was a wound in his calf that poured blood, and his trouser leg and shoe were sodden.

"Doesn't matter," he said. "Can't feel it."

"Your dad's nice," Sparky said.

Reaper was walking slowly along the street, his shadow dancing beside him as he passed the flaming wreck. The fire had spread to the houses' structures now, and smoke was seeping from the roofs of buildings several doors along. Soon, the whole terrace would go up.

"I can't give up on him," Jack said.

"Jack, he could kill you." Jenna stepped forward and held his face in her hands, and he saw the pity in her eyes. He *hated* that.

"But he won't." Jack ran along the street after his father, and he heard his friends coming along behind him.

Reaper had reached the first downed helicopter, where his Superiors were flanking Miller and two surviving soldiers. The soldiers each nursed a broken arm, and looked around in obvious terror.

"Miller," Reaper said. "It's been a long time since we were face to face."

"And I remember what happened then," Miller said.

Reaper smiled and lifted his shirt, displaying an ugly, bubbled scar across his stomach and hip. "Smarted for a bit," he said, nodding. "But I'm much stronger now. Just ask your barbequed friends."

Miller glanced along the street toward the burning helicopter, then he saw Jack, and his eyes went wide.

"Dad, Emily was here too," Jack said. "But she's gone. We found Mum and they've left together, and I want you to leave too."

"With you?" Reaper asked.

"Yes," Jack nodded. "Dad . . ." He could not hold back a tear, and he wiped it angrily from his cheek. "Mum's given up on you. She says you're . . . too far gone."

Reaper held up his hands and turned around, looking at the rooks still circling, the fire spreading along the street, the Superiors standing casually around the captured Chopper and his two soldiers. "Why would I ever want to give all this up?"

"They want you to join with them," Jack said. "Break out of London."

Reaper waved a dismissive hand. "I know they do. But they have no vision, no ambition, and no idea of what's coming."

"And you do?"

"Of course." He pointed at Miller. "First, this bastard gets his comeuppance. Not sure quite how yet, but we Superiors are imaginative. Then after that . . . well, that's for me to know, not you."

"I'm your son!"

Reaper smiled sarcastically. "What's your name, again?"

Sparky and Jenna were behind him, and Jenna touched his arm. "We should go," she whispered.

"I'm not leaving yet," Jack said. "Lucy-Anne?"

Lucy-Anne looked at her three friends from across the other side of the circle, stepping closer to the bird-boy as she did so. "My brother's still alive somewhere," she said, and her voice sounded different. Older? Wiser? Jack wasn't certain. *Changed*, for sure. "Rook said he'll help me find him. And there's something . . ." Lucy-Anne trailed off, frowning, and then several rooks fluttered down and landed on her shoulders. She grimaced for a couple of seconds; then she looked at Jack and smiled.

"Say your goodbyes, Chopper bastard," Reaper said. The blind Superior drew a throwing knife and knelt, drawing her arm back ready to unleash the weapon.

"They didn't get out," Miller said, kneeling and raising a hand in useless defence. "Emily and your mother, Jack . . . we caught them in the tunnels. The other Irregular put up quite a fight for an old woman. We have them in Camp H, and if anything happens to me . . ."

Reaper muttered something, and the Superior held her throwing stance.

"You have ten seconds," Reaper said. "And I'm only giving you that because you mentioned the camp."

"You know all about it!" Miller said. "It's where we take you freaks when we want to cut your brains out, slice and dice them and examine them under—"

"You call it Camp Hope," Reaper growled.

A shadow streaked out from behind the fallen aircraft, denying the sun its rightful touch, and Miller flipped backward as something struck him in the face. The shadow was a man, standing beside the Chopper and leaning down, his hand raised for another blow.

"I don't like being called a freak," the shadow man said.

"Leave him, Shade," Reaper said. "I've just thought of a nicer way for him to die."

"The soldiers at Camp H are angry," Miller said, staring directly at Jack and ignoring the blood on his own face. "They've all lost friends these past couple of days, and I'm a friend to them all. There's no saying what they'll do to your mother and sister before they kill them."

"Dad," Jack said. "Reaper. *Please!* He has Mum and Emily."

"I don't know those names," the Superior said, but this time he did not meet Jack's gaze.

"But I do," Jack said. "And whether you recognise them anymore or not, you wouldn't kill your own wife and daughter, would you? After everything that's happened?"

Reaper stared at Miller, who stared at Jack. Jack shivered. A rook cried out and Lucy-Anne shifted slightly, a bird on her head fluttering away as though called somewhere else.

"Please, Dad," Jack said, lifting his voice above the roar of the spreading flames. The air was redolent with the stench of cooking flesh, and he felt sick. But he had not come this far to lose everything, and everything now rested on his father's shoulders.

On *Reaper's* shoulders.

"Those two," Reaper said quietly, and a blink later the soldiers either side of Miller both slumped to the ground with knives protruding from their throats. One of them gurgled and clutched at the blade with his good arm, but the blind Superior's aim had been true, and they died quickly.

Miller gasped and stood up, staring defiantly into Reaper's eyes.

"Ready?" Reaper said, grinning. Miller did not respond.

"You're a monster," Jack hissed. "A beast, worse than him, worse than *all* the Choppers. You can save people who love you, here and now. But what do you choose, Dad?"

His father did not react. Jack felt movement around him, and he knew that Shade was somewhere close by, ready to strike.

"*Reaper!* What a name. Who chose that? You should be wearing your underpants on the outside and have a good reserve of one-liners." Jack snorted. "You're dressed in black, I'll give you that."

"Don't mock me, child!" his father cried, and Jack gasped at the effect of his father's voice. It struck him like something solid, knocking air from his lungs and sweeping his legs from beneath him. Jack hit the ground on one arm, managing not to cry out at the sudden pain.

But Reaper was frowning at him now, and there was something going on in his mind other than violence. Jack could see it. He could *sense* it. And as he closed his eyes, he felt his father's confusion as past struggled with present, to define the future.

He *felt* it.

*I can feel what he's thinking!* Jack thought, and the taste of the Nomad's finger flooded his mouth. But now was no time for wonder.

"Your friends?" Reaper asked, nodding at Sparky and Jenna.

"Yes. My friends."

"Ten minutes."

"What do you mean?" Jack asked, standing slowly.

"You have ten minutes. I'll wait here with my friend Miller, chat to him, perhaps try and persuade him to tell me a few things I've been wondering about for some time. And in ten minutes I'll let him go. By then his people will be coming for him, and they'll be after you. All of them." He nodded at the Chopper, looking him up and down like a cut of meat. "And look at him. He's hungry for you."

"We think Nomad touched him," Miller whispered. He looked at Jack, and Jack could taste the Nomad, and feel the excitement in the Chopper's mind as if it were his own. *He sees something in me.*

"There is no Nomad," Reaper said.

"You of all people—"

"She's a myth!" Reaper whispered, a terrible sound.

"I lured you in," Miller said to Jack. "That nice picture of your mother?" He feigned taking a photograph. "And I thought you would be enough, but now that you've been touched by *her* . . ." He was amazed, and terrified, and there was suddenly so much more Jack needed to know.

Jack ran his tongue around his mouth. And deep inside he could feel a dreadful, wonderful change already beginning.

"Dad, please will you—"

Reaper glared at him, and there wasn't a hint of anything other than malice in his eyes. "Nine minutes, fifty seconds."

"You're not my father," Jack said, and Reaper only shrugged.

"Come on, Jack," Jenna said.

But there was one more thing to try, one last time. "Lucy-Anne, are you sure?"

She shook her head and drew closer to Rook. "My brother. But I'll do my best to dream the best for you."

Jack frowned, because he did not understand. But at least the guilt of leaving Lucy-Anne had been lifted from his shoulders. And it was a good thing, because the responsibility already weighing on him would crush him, given half a chance.

"Jack," Sparky said. He and Jenna were already retreating along the street.

"Nine minutes, forty seconds."

Jack walked quickly through the line of Superiors—the blind knife-thrower, the shadow man, Reaper—until he was standing face to face with Miller. The man's eye and nose were bleeding, but he did not flinch.

"Rosemary is yours," Jack said.

Miller snorted, shook his head. "I don't conspire with freaks."

"*Someone's* been giving us away."

Miller only shrugged.

"Fair enough," Jack said. "But if Reaper does what he says and decides to let you go, remember this: I swear, before everyone standing here, that if you or any of your scumbag friends lay a hand on my mother or sister, I will fucking kill you."

Miller blinked and looked down at his feet.

"Nine minutes, twenty seconds," Reaper muttered.

"All right!" Jack shouted, spinning and walking past his father. "We're going!"

He followed Sparky and Jenna as they jogged along the street, and every fibre of him was screaming to look back. But he and Lucy-

Anne had said their goodbyes. Miller had Jack's vow fresh in his mind. And his father . . .

His father was dead.

*Nine minutes*, Jack heard as they rounded a corner and ran, the three of them sprinting as fast as they could. They passed dead things and living things that had fed on the dead. They smelled cooking meat on the air from the people they had just seen killed. They had no idea where to go next.

Still running, Jack pulled the bloodstained photograph from his jeans pocket. Knowing it had been taken by Miller or his Choppers made it feel tainted. He turned it over, felt around its edges, his suspicion already hardening into certainty. And without actually feeling or touching it, he sensed the small metal square cast into one corner of the card. It was like a smell in his mind, a taste on his vision. He ripped the photo in half, ignoring the sight of his mother's face cut in two.

"What're you doing?" Sparky panted.

Jack tore and tore again, then held up the thin metal device. He did not have to tell either of his friends what it was.

The sound of helicopters grew in the distance, and Jack threw the tracking chip through a smashed shop window.

Once the hunters, now the hunted, the three friends ran deeper into the Toxic City.

When the ten minutes were up, still they ran. Helicopters buzzed overhead, motors echoed around street corners, and they were the centre of attention.

The pain in Jack's injured ankle was awful, and as he ran, the Nomad's taste came to him again. The pain ended, and he coughed up something that looked like black rice. Spitting it out, he wondered, *What the hell's happening to me?* But really he knew.

Sparky lifted a grating in the pavement outside an old greengrocer's, and Jack and Jenna slid down the steep chute. Sparky lowered the grating and followed them down.

In the darkness, they huddled together at the rear of the basement. It was empty and unused, and there was the faint scent of old decay from one dark corner. They kept away from it; they had seen enough dead things.

"You think it was only that photo?" Sparky asked.

"We'll soon find out," Jack said. He felt so lost and alone, and he could not help imagining what Emily and his mother were going through right now. Whenever he blinked, he was presented with terrible possibilities: Emily strapped down with probes being driven into her eyes; his mother on her back, chest plate cracked, and her heart beating in her open chest. He wanted to cry and rage at the visions, but he knew that for now, silence was their friend.

And now he felt different inside, constantly changing, an astounding potential swelling so large that he was surprised he did not burst apart. *I know things*, he thought. *I can see things*. He looked at his hands and knew they could heal. When he blinked, he saw constellations of power across the insides of his eyelids. The Nomad had seeded a change within him, but he was not yet sure how he could tell Sparky and Jenna.

"So what now?" Jenna asked.

"Now, we rescue Emily and my mum."

"Damn right!" Sparky said.

"And then home," Jenna sighed.

"No." Jack shook his head. "And then back into the city."

"But—"

"Jenna, if you had a chance to rescue your father from what he's become, would you take it?"

"You think there's really a chance?" Jenna asked, and Jack looked away, because the possible answers to that question were tearing him apart.

"I can't ask you both—" he began, but Sparky punched his arm and grabbed him in a headlock.

"You even *suggest* we leave you on your own, and I'll break your neck," his friend growled.

Something drove along the street. The vehicle skidded to a halt, and boots thumped the pavement. "Every house," someone shouted in the distance, "every room, every basement!"

"Oh, hell, that's not good," Sparky said, letting Jack go.

"It'll be okay." A curious calm settled over Jack, and every time he remembered Nomad's face, and tasted her finger in his mouth, the calmness intensified. He closed his eyes and breathed deep. When he opened them again, someone was sliding down the chute into the basement.

Torchlight probed the darkness.

"Still and quiet," Jack whispered, holding his two friends' hands.

The soldier was just a shadow behind his heavy torch, a silhouette spiked with weapons and breathing heavily with fear, or excitement.

Jack closed his eyes and opened his mind, and instinct found something new.

"What the hell—"

"Torch hit me right across my eyes, and—"

"As if we were invisible!"

Jack hushed them both. "Nomad touched me," he said.

"The first vector!" Jenna gasped.

"And still contagious. I feel *so much*. My senses, broadening. I know things I shouldn't. Not just one thing, but many. It's scary." But even he knew that his voice did not sound afraid.

It sounded *exhilarated.*

They waited in the basement while the searching Choppers melted away into the distance.

And later, when Jack and his friends started making plans, he saw the careful glances they cast his way, and he sensed their unease.

As if he was no longer the Jack they used to know.

# ABOUT THE AUTHOR

TIM LEBBON is a *New York Times*–bestselling writer from South Wales. He's had over twenty novels published to date, as well as dozens of novellas and hundreds of short stories. Recent books include the first two volumes of *The Secret Journeys of Jack London* trilogy (co-authored with Christopher Golden), *Coldbrook*, and *The Heretic Land*. *London Eye* is his first solo YA novel. He has won four British Fantasy Awards, a Bram Stoker Award, and a Scribe Award, and has been a finalist for World Fantasy, International Horror Guild, and Shirley Jackson Awards.

Fox 2000 have acquired film rights to *The Secret Journeys of Jack London*, and several more of his novels and novellas are currently in development. He is working on several screenplays, solo and in collaboration, as well as new novel projects.

Find out more about Tim at his website www.timlebbon.net.